Assassin

Tomos James

Assassin

Olympia Publishers
London

www.olympiapublishers.com
OLYMPIA PAPERBACK EDITION

Copyright © Tomos James 2023

The right of Tomos James to be identified as author of
this work has been asserted in accordance with sections 77 and 78 of
the Copyright, Designs and Patents Act 1988.

All Rights Reserved

No reproduction, copy or transmission of this publication
may be made without written permission.
No paragraph of this publication may be reproduced,
copied or transmitted save with the written permission of the publisher,
or in accordance with the provisions
of the Copyright Act 1956 (as amended).

Any person who commits any unauthorised act in relation to
this publication may be liable to criminal
prosecution and civil claims for damage.

A CIP catalogue record for this title is
available from the British Library.

ISBN: 978-1-80439-092-4

This is a work of fiction.
Names, characters, places and incidents originate from the writer's
imagination. Any resemblance to actual persons, living or dead, is
purely coincidental.

First Published in 2023

Olympia Publishers
Tallis House
2 Tallis Street
London
EC4Y 0AB

Printed in Great Britain

Prologue

The target would be along any minute now if my intel was good. I checked the rifle once more and looked through the sight. Sure enough, he rounded the corner almost exactly as expected. It was an easier job when you had good information. Planning was more simplistic. I composed myself and lined up the shot. Hit the target and get out without being seen was the brief. Basic. It was satisfying to see how arrogant he looked and therefore I knew I would enjoy my work more. I entered into "the zone". All other thoughts removed, only concentration on the job in hand. I'd heard of the phrase "concentration is the absence of irrelevant thought" and was aware how, at these moments, I could focus on just what I needed to. The world appeared silent and serene, as though everything had halted whilst I carried out my work. I started to put pressure on the trigger, his head perfectly in my sight. I enjoyed the moment just before the hit the most. I didn't want it to end and knew that I had the propensity to push it to the limit, potentially endangering success. I held the moment a couple more seconds. Then, difficult to tell looking back, either he made the slightest movement or I anticipated he was about to move and I increased the pressure. Within a couple of seconds, he was lying on the ground and all hell was breaking loose. This was the part I liked least. Getting out of there. It required a complete change of state. I made my way across the buildings and eventually down into the streets. Within fifteen minutes, I was a long way from the scene and judged myself safe. I allowed myself a smile. I loved my job.

Chapter One

Looking back, I was a completely different person on the night my story begins. There are many possible reasons I chose the path that dramatically changed my life. I was twenty-two and bored with life. I didn't really enjoy my job, labouring for a small building company that paid poorly and couldn't always guarantee me work. I also still lived with my parents, desperately wanting to move out, but unable to due to a lack of money. My life was drifting and up until that point I'd been too lazy to do anything about it.

Another thing that would have been weighing on my mind at the time was the ending of the closest thing I'd had to a serious relationship. I never openly admitted at the time that this was troubling me and even struggled to accept it myself. I was too proud to let the emotion of losing a girlfriend get on top of me, even though, looking back, it clearly had.

My social life was the one thing that kept me going. I was living for Friday and Saturday nights. All the money I earned seemed to be spent in pubs and clubs. I, like many people my age, had a great circle of friends. Most of them were old school friends, but I'd also acquired friends through work and just by meeting people in my local pub. The Crooked Billet pub was the hub of my social life. I'd got to know many of the people that drank in there and it was where I was happiest. My friends and I did go to other pubs as well as clubs, but generally that was where we started our nights out. When I went out on a Friday or

Saturday night, I wouldn't have to pre-arrange to meet anyone, I'd just turn up at the pub and there'd always be a few of my mates occupying the place already. I thought drinking was great and I couldn't get drunk enough. If I'd been told at the time that I'd drink myself to an early death, it wouldn't have bothered me. In fact, I'd have considered it cool. In my eyes, drinking heavily was macho and it impressed the people that mattered to me. Strangely enough, my new career would take me away from this life of excessive alcohol.

Outside of my social world of drinking, I didn't care or certainly didn't want to care about life. Nothing else interested me. The problems of other people were irrelevant, or something to laugh about down the pub. I liked the idea of being cold, emotionless, and aloof. It made me feel stronger as a person. I considered being emotionally tough as good as, if not better than, being physically tough.

My life, therefore, consisted of regularly getting drunk, occasionally dabbling in drugs, and waiting for something to happen. I hadn't been prepared to do anything about the things I was unhappy about in my life. It was almost as though I knew something would come up, something that would allow me to enjoy life more as well as bring me money. It's strange how at that age you're so optimistic about the future, even if you're not prepared to work hard to set a foundation for it. Despite not having any real intentions of getting off my backside to do anything about my general discontent for life, something did crop up for me. It was something that would make my life dangerous, exciting, and individual, as well as provide me with a very good income. It was the sort of thing I'd fantasise about before it happened.

The night it began was a Friday in the Crooked Billet. Just

like any other, I was drinking with my mates, celebrating the end of another working week. There was a guy there called H; I never did discover his real name. He'd been a regular in the pub for some time. He didn't seem to have any mates he went there with, but he knew a lot of the people who drank in there to talk to. He'd occupy the bar at the far end of the pub, usually on a stool, cigarette in hand, either talking to another regular or just surveying the pub. Recently, he'd taken to coming over and talking to my crowd. I don't know how it had started, but like most people I'd got to know in there other than my initial friends, it was probably through a chat at the bar whilst waiting to be served or a drunken exchange in the toilets about a barmaid just before closing time. My group of mates generally occupied the area around the pillar in the centre of the pub. When I walked in it would be the first place I'd scan for familiar faces. H was older than me, probably in his late twenties. I knew very little about him in reality. We'd laugh about drunken experiences, or girls we'd pulled or failed with. I remember he was into football big time, something that didn't interest me. He'd go on about the hooliganism side of it and how much he enjoyed that aspect of it. We didn't question him or in our minds about the morality of this, we just liked listening to the tales he told us of people he'd beaten up and the run ins he had with the police. You could tell he loved having an audience and got off on telling us his stories of violence. He wasn't a huge guy, although quite sturdy, but he had an aura and intensity about him that made you know you shouldn't mess with him.

He seemed to permanently have stubble around a misshapen mouth that was always extra animated when relaying one of his stories. He had a couple of small scars he boasted he obtained during his football clashes. If I met him now, I would certainly not want to befriend him. However, being young and impressionable, I liked him at the time. He was entertaining and seemed to have time for me and my mates, and therefore we started talking to him regularly. I remember that we'd talked about killing people for a living before that night. It had been in a light-hearted manner, but H had mentioned how many people were always looking to have someone killed. He talked about how people got in your way during life and removing them or having them removed could often make things simpler. Scarred lovers seeking revenge, rival businesses, police grasses, someone you hold a grudge against for a past offence or even insurance jobs. He had also talked about the market rate for having somebody taken out.

This particular night the subject came up again, I can't recall exactly how. It was just me and H talking. Naturally I was there with other mates, but they were talking amongst themselves, oblivious to my conversation. I questioned H more on the subject, sensing he may have somehow got involved in this racket in the past, given the way he talked about it. Suddenly he was asking me more about my life, what I did, was I happy in my job and with the money I earned. He said, if I was interested, he could get me real work that paid proper money. It would drastically change my life for the better. He said that not many people were cut out for it, but that he saw in me a quality required for the job. Naive and slow on the uptake, I didn't immediately grasp what he was suggesting, I was just listening to him, intrigued. He had a way of holding my attention when he talked; he'd look me in the eye and speak with a real intensity, his mouth moving far more than necessary to form the words he wanted to say. I was wondering what it was he wanted me to do, him believing I'd be good at it, already convincing me I'd be a natural even though I'd failed to work out what it was. Then it clicked; it was no ordinary work. I suspected it would be illegal, drug dealing, burglary, but what he was asking me to become was a professional hit man. How he knew that I'd be great at it or that he could trust me I had no idea. After all, he'd known me less than a few months and all we'd had were mostly drunken conversations in a group. As far as I could recall, he'd never questioned me about my life outside the pub before that night. Maybe he'd had me followed, not that this would have given him much of a clue as to whether I was up to it. Perhaps it was just some gut instinct he had. He was right though; I didn't know it at the time, but I could do it and he could trust me. Maybe he didn't have anything to lose, after all, if I'd gone to the police the next day, they probably wouldn't have believed me, and I wouldn't have had any evidence to back up my accusation. Not that going to the police occurred to me. The only question I had was whether to accept his offer or not.

Whilst we were talking it hadn't felt like we were still in the pub. The rest of the pub seemed surreal, removed from us. It was as though H and I had been beamed into another world. A world we'd stay in until the conversation ended. Thinking about it afterwards, I would have expected to believe at the time that he was winding me up, just having a laugh at my expense. I did have my doubts but the way he was, the seriousness he had about him and the business-like manner he discussed the matter with convinced me it was real.

"You really think I could make a living knocking people off," I blurted out, when finally realising what he meant.

He gave a sincere yes. He then continued talking about how dull he thought my current life must be, that all I did was drink in this pub and that his offer was a way to escape the misery of it. This offended me to a point, him belittling me and my life, but deep down I knew he was right. I was offended more because I knew that it was the truth; I was going nowhere, I had nothing, and I needed to do something with my life.

H made a point of saying things like "you only get one chance in life", "make the most of it and don't worry about everyone else", "just look after yourself". He said he could put me in touch with someone to set the ball rolling. He'd convinced me sufficiently. I wanted to take him up on his offer.

"Of course," he said at the end of his talk, "if you don't think you're up to it and want to keep on plodding along doing what you're doing, then no problem, we can forget this little conversation ever happened. You'll probably regret it though."

I rose to the bait. How could I turn down such an opportunity to change my life and become someone? An assassin, it sounded great, like the guy in the film *Leon*. It would be cool. I was probably a little pissed at the time, but H had built up an extra euphoria in me. I had that excited feeling in my stomach, the sort that curbs your hunger. I really wanted to do it, but knew I had to mull it over first, sleep on it.

"I'm really interested, though I'm going to have to think about it," I said.

"No problem," he replied.

"Tell me how it works then," I asked.

"Well, if you do decide to do it, all you need to do is set up a P.O. Box address."

I looked at H to see if he was taking the piss when he said this, but he looked deadly serious.

"Then I give you a number to ring," he continued, "you phone it, leave a message with the P.O. Box address and a contact number to ring. Then you await further instructions."

H paused and I started to ask my next question, one of

numerous I had floating around my head on the whole matter.

"You have to remember though," H interrupted me, "that once you leave that message with your address, you've bought in. No going back."

I didn't like the way H said this. But I needed to hear it. It made me realise what I could potentially be getting myself into. Even though I was partially deterred by this, I continued questioning him.

"So, what happens after I phone with the address?"

"When a job comes up, you'll get a call or instructions will be left at the address. Jobs can be anywhere, up north, abroad. It's better that way, you don't want to have to take someone out who lives in your street."

"How do I go about doing it?" I asked.

H laughed at this. This was the first time his mood had changed from seriousness since the start of the conversation.

"That's up to you, mate," he said with a grin. I didn't speak for a minute whilst I digested this information. Hearing it had brough me back down to earth a bit. I had visions of being given a date and a time, as well as a weapon to do it, but this didn't seem the case. H studied me whilst I was having these thoughts. I knew he was judging whether he still thought I could do it, looking for signs in my facial expressions as to how I was taking this in and whether I believed I could do it.

I ended the lull in the conversation. "So, where, when, how doesn't matter then?" Even though I knew the answer to this, I wanted confirmation. H shook his head from side to side, his eyes on mine the whole time, checking me out, almost challenging me.

"What do I get for it?" I asked. A quizzical look fell over his face. But then, as though someone had switched something on, his expression changed once more, to a knowing look.

"Money, you mean?"

"Yep."

"Don't know, mate. It varies from job to job, circumstances etc. You find out with the instructions." He stopped, and then as an afterthought said, "Not that it means it's negotiable or you can go back once you're committed."

I didn't like the way it was going. Some of the earlier euphoria had dissipated and I was internally debating whether to pull the plug on the idea before I took it any further. H had become aloof and this talk of "once you're in, you're in" was putting me off.

"The money's good though, right?" I asked, more trying to convince myself it was worth doing than anything else.

"Of course," he replied, still not elaborating.

I wanted to ask him if he did it: killed people for a living. I, after all, had no idea what he did. But I couldn't ask him. It's difficult to explain why, but somehow it didn't seem right, not in line with the etiquette of the world we were talking in. I wondered whether he was just a middleman, setting things up, or whether he was killing people for money as well. I pondered over his life. He pulled a cigarette packet from his pocket and offered me one. I didn't really like the brand he had but I took one anyway. He lit the cigarette with a gold plated lighter, and then proceeded to rip the inner paper from the cigarette packet.

"Do you wanna pint?" he asked me.

I nodded.

"Lager?"

"Yeah, cheers."

He went to the bar, leaving me standing there alone. He'd been so casual asking me if I wanted a drink. It was weird after the discussion we'd just had, as though it hadn't really happened, or we'd just been talking about what was on television last night. I stood there in a bit of a daze for a while, trying to take in what had just been said. Looking around the pub, everybody else's conversation seemed insignificant. They were ignorant of the things H and I had just spoke about and this made me feel more important than them.

H was back with a pint quickly, even though the area around the bar was crowded with people trying to get served. He had somehow managed it straight away. He handed me the pint. He'd been busy at the bar, not just with being served, because he then slipped me the piece of paper he'd torn from his cigarette packet.

"I recommend you ring it, mate," he said, eyeing the paper as I looked at the phone number he'd written on it. He said this in a friendly, almost brotherly way. As though he was giving me one of the most important pieces of advice I could ever receive. I put the paper in my pocket, dilemma already raging in my head as to whether to take his advice or not. After this, we stood there sipping our pints in silence for what have could not have been longer than a minute before he said he wanted to speak to a guy he knew over the other side of the pub. He moved off, pushing his way through the crowd, leaving me once again in deep contemplation. A few moments later, I forced myself away from my thoughts and re-joined my mates. I'd have to think it over again in the morning when I had a clear head and the dust had settled on the matter. Although, I knew then that I'd not feel any differently on the subject the next day. There was going to be no obvious answer that would spring to mind when I woke up.

My mates would have found me quiet for the rest of that evening. I was normally quite vocal in the pub after a few drinks, especially on a Friday. I loved the buzz of a pub on a Friday night, everyone on a high with the prospect of a weekend ahead. My mates went on to the local nightclub afterwards. I declined to go despite furious persuasions. I wouldn't have gone even if I hadn't had that discussion with H. I didn't have the cash.

I walked home, not wanting to bother with waiting for a taxi. I wasn't in a real rush to be home anyway. It took about an hour, but I enjoyed the time on my own thinking over the conversation I'd had with H earlier.

I didn't think about anything else over the weekend. I can recall staring at the phone number H had written down for me in my bedroom. I knew that I had to ring it, but at the same time the thought scared me. It felt like the opportunity of a lifetime, although I had doubts that I could go through with it. The real temptation to me was the image. It was the ultimate cool job, even if I did picture it like being a character in a poor American film. Me dressed all in black, lying on a rooftop, looking through the sight of a rifle at a target, finger ready to squeeze the trigger. I thought there'd be no buzz like it. I was aware this was a simplistic outlook of what I would be doing, but, even so, I craved the glamour of doing it. The money wasn't a major thing to me. I'd like it and could do with a few extra quid in my pocket at the end of the month, but I wasn't materialistic. Moving out of home and having the cash to get drunk whenever I wanted would be sufficient.

Chapter Two

The first positive step I took towards changing my career was when my sister was over visiting me the Sunday after I'd spoken to H. She's a couple of years older than me and had moved out to live with her boyfriend the year before. She was pregnant at the time. We didn't get on at all when we were younger. We fought and argued like hell and never saw eye to eye. I wouldn't say we'd grown close at the time, but we did get on better. She'd miscarried her baby and, although upset by the event, I reckon it actually made her a better person. Maybe it made her think about life more. I'm not certain she really wanted it anyway.

We were sitting in the living room, watching some boring film on the television. My mum was in the kitchen washing up the dishes and my dad was dozing in the armchair; a typical Sunday afternoon scene at our house. I asked my sister how you set up a P.O. Box. She looked at me in a weird way and answered that she wasn't sure but supposed that you did it at the post office. I responded to her questioning that I had a mate who'd asked me the same thing. Therefore, despite still having major doubts, my plan was to go to the post office the following day and set the ball rolling.

I went to the Billet again that Sunday night. I probably would have gone there anyway, but I wanted to see H again. I didn't have anything specific to ask him, I just wanted reassurance that it was real. I stood in the pub talking to my mates. However, most of the time I wasn't really concentrating on the conversation;

instead, I was regularly looking over to where H was. He was sat in his usual spot at the bar, but unlike most recent times I'd been in there, he didn't come over for a chat. I continued looking over towards him as the night drew to an end. As closing time was imminent, I realised he wasn't going to wander over to where we were. I couldn't let the night pass without speaking to him. Him ignoring me added to my paranoia on the subject, wondering if it was real and not some practical joke. I went to the toilet which was closer to where he was sitting. On my way out of the toilet I went over to where he was. He greeted me but didn't seem overly happy to see me. I made small talk with him and another guy he'd been talking to for a short time, before his friend wandered off. I didn't waste time bringing up the subject we'd spoke about on Friday.

"I'm going to the post office tomorrow to set up a P.O. Box."

"Good," H replied, but looked away.

"When I phone the number, will it be you who gets the message?"

"No, but listen, never ask questions about who else is involved in this."

"OK." I agreed. "They'll know who I am though when I ring yeah?"

"Yes," H replied, but he had irritation in his voice. He looked uncomfortable with the subject, not like he had been on Friday. I dropped the matter, realising this is what he wanted me to do. I went back to my mates a few minutes later. I would have been disheartened by our conversation had it not been for the way we'd parted. I told him I was off and started walking away when he called my name. I looked back at him; his eyes stared deep into mine. This was the friendliest he'd been to me since I'd gone over to him.

"Good luck, mate," was all he said. But it was spoken with such sincerity that it instantly made me feel better. He'd looked like he had on the Friday when we were discussing the subject and his words were said with conviction. It was how you'd expect a proud father to speak to his son before something major was due to happen in his life. I was going to go through with it. I speculated after as to why H had been like he had. Perhaps now he knew that it was likely I was going to get involved, he didn't want to speak to me. It may have been from a security point of view. My theory was certainly backed up by the fact I never spoke to him again after this.

The Monday morning feeling the next day fuelled my desire to do it. At lunch time, rather than go with my work mates to get something to eat, I made my excuses and headed for the post office. There was one not too far from the building site where I was working at the time. As I'd anticipated, the queue was very long. I should have known that it wouldn't be a simple process. Firstly, I had to fill out a form, then I had to provide proof of my current address through certain documentation. On top of this was a fee, which I'd naively not considered beforehand, for creating the P.O. Box. Lastly, the process could take as long as two weeks. I walked away from the post office dejectedly, cursing why nothing was ever simple. In retrospect, I can't believe I felt a sense of injustice at the fact that it would take me two weeks and a small amount of administration to create a process whereby I could earn lots of money taking people's lives.

I lost impetus on the task in the next couple of days, the extra effort required to set up the P.O. Box knocking me back. I still had intentions of doing it, but was putting off the boring task of form filing and finding the necessary paperwork. This reflected a strong personality trait of mine at the time - laziness.

On Wednesday evening that week, I stopped at the newsagents on my way back from work to buy some fags. Coming out of the shop I bumped into my ex-girlfriend. We hadn't split up on bad terms, although I hadn't fully understood why she'd ended it. She talked to me in a friendly manner and seemed happy to see me. I thought back to our last conversation. It was thirty-three days ago. We were sitting in her car after a night out at the cinema followed by a quick drink in the pub. She was dropping me off at my house and we were parked outside. I should have suspected something when at the beginning of the night she told me that she had to be up early the next morning and therefore didn't want me to stay at her house, something I did regularly. It had been a normal evening from what I recall. We hadn't argued or had any kind of disagreement. We sat outside my house in her car, a silence fell on our conversation. I was just about to kiss her goodnight before getting out. Her words were clear, but I couldn't make sense of it.

"I think we should end this." I turned my head towards her sharply, a sinking feeling in my stomach.

"What…why?"

"It's difficult to explain, but I just don't think it's working. It's time to move on." She said this in a caring way, her words soft; she knew the subject was delicate and I could tell she was worried about my reaction.

Her explanation never really expanded on these words and standing outside the shop, I still didn't understand. Not least why she'd let us have a perfectly normal evening together knowing she was going to terminate our relationship at the end of it. I loved her much more than I wanted to, not that I told her. Ideally, I'd forget about her and move on. Whilst we were in our relationship, I knew I was in too deep and that I'd probably get hurt. I never told anyone how much I felt for her. My mates saw it as a casual relationship and my family didn't even know she existed beyond fielding the occasional phone call from her. Emotions were a weakness in my mind and I wanted to crush them. I couldn't even fully communicate to her that night, when I was trying to talk her out of ending it, how much I liked her. She'd made up her mind though. As far as I could gather there wasn't anyone else. She said she still liked me and alluded to the fact that maybe if we stayed in touch we could try again sometime. This further perplexed me. My reaction to it since then had been to go out as much as possible and get drunk. Hardly any of my family or mates had met her. I hadn't made the effort to introduce her to them and kept the two apart. She'd mentioned this at the end when I was trying to talk her out of it. Although, it wasn't like she'd asked to meet them. Talking to her outside the newsagents, I wanted to beg her to get back with me, but I kept my pride intact. She seemed happy with life, which I resented, but at the same time made me want to improve mine. I wanted to compete with her and prove to myself I was happier than her. Maybe even make her envious of what I had and then regret leaving me. I learned she'd just got a new job which paid well by all accounts. We parted awkwardly, neither of us really knowing what to say to the other, me still harbouring unrealistic hopes that maybe we would get together again at some point. After this conversation I did know that I had to do something with my life. H was right, it was boring.

    Over the next couple of days, I got my act together and filled in the post office form, dug out a recent bank statement I'd stuffed into a drawer in my bedroom, and was back down the post office by the end of the week. I'd even managed to borrow a small amount of money from a mate to cover the charge of having a

P.O. Box, not that I'd told him what it was for. I now felt much better about things and waited impatiently for the post office to respond. Because of my cash situation, I tried to curb the amount of time I spent in the Crooked Billet over the next few days, but naturally found myself in there a couple of times over the weekend. I did see H in there once, but again he made no effort to come over. I didn't go over to see him either, put off by the response I received last time. It was now obvious to me he wanted to keep a distance and I was ready to respect that, even though I could have asked him several questions given the opportunity. Even one of my mates commented on how unsociable he'd become. I didn't respond. I had regular thoughts as to why this was. Maybe H keeping his distance meant this whole thing was real, as now he'd set it up, he'd taken a step back and no longer wanted to be seen with me to protect us. On the other hand, it could just be that he'd had his fun with me and was no longer interested.

Chapter Three

It was the next Wednesday after I arrived home from work that I saw I had a letter from the post office. The letter set off emotions immediately; it was another step in the process. With my heart beating faster and a sense of fear, I stared at the envelope flicking it over to examine it. Even though I do it, it always amazes me how people stare at letters before opening them, looking for clues as to who it's from and what it will say. It's obvious that the best way to find out is just to open it straight away rather than looking at it, but the more mysterious the letter, the longer people seem to stare at it before opening. I opened it and saw confirmation my P.O. Box address had been set up and was ready for use. I could collect the mail from my box at the local post office. They'd turned it around much quicker than the two weeks they told me to allow. The letter made me feel as though I'd started a process I couldn't stop, as though I wasn't in control. This was obviously wrong, as by not ringing the number yet I hadn't committed to anything, but somehow creating the P.O. Box made me feel as though I'd signed up for it.

It was another three days before I brought myself to ring the number. I'd been in the Crooked Billet the night before, two weeks after my conversation with H. He wasn't in there that night, but I constantly looked over to where he usually sat, expecting him to appear at any moment. The next morning, I sat in my bedroom, tired and hungover. I hadn't slept that well; there'd been much on my mind. I was trying to psyche myself up to go and ring the number. I was playing a compilation CD and listened to one song which began with the lyric, "It's better to regret something you have done than something you haven't done." I thought about this line, working out what it meant. It was something that gave me the little extra push to go through with making the call.

I didn't want to call the number from home. Our only phone was in the hallway downstairs and I would be at the risk of one of my parents hearing me. I didn't want this extra worry. Instead, after a quick panic trying to locate the number H had given me, I traipsed off to a phone box just down the road from where I lived. I was on a mission and even though I was as nervous as hell, dry in the throat and severely doubting my actions, I was determined to go through with it.

I stood in the phone box, staring at the number, recalling H's instructions to leave the P.O. Box details and a phone number. I had to leave my home number, not something I really wanted to do as my parents would more than likely pick up the call, but I had no choice. However, I knew that if this panned out into what I hoped it might, I'd soon have enough cash to move out. Another smaller concern I had was that I'd have to talk to an answer machine, not something I liked doing. It didn't seem right talking to a machine. Pushing that aside, I rehearsed in my head what I'd say. I'd already done this several times since I'd originally spoke to H. I dialled the number, partly hoping it would be engaged or unattainable, giving me a valid excuse for giving up. It connected and I heard the ringing tone. It rang four times; I was beginning to wonder if someone would answer and if they did, what would I say to them? Suddenly, I heard a click and the beginning of a recorded message. It was an automated voice that simply said leave a message after the beep. My heart was beating fast and I knew I was going to have trouble speaking clearly. The beep went; I paused for what was probably only a couple of seconds, this was my last chance to pull out, but I didn't hang up. I stuttered and stumbled my way to a message that left only my name, P.O. Box address and phone number as I'd been instructed. Once finished, I replaced the handset and leant my head against it. I had a huge sinking feeling in my stomach. I felt nauseous and sick, all I could think is, "what have I done?" I'd really wanted to make the call and go through with it, but now I'd done it, I instantly regretted it. I'd just committed myself to killing people. I stayed in the phone box for a couple of minutes after I'd ended the call. Eventually I stepped out. As I walked home slowly, completely unaware of anything happening around me, H's words were ringing in my head, "You have to remember though that once you leave the message with your address, you've bought in." What had I bought into? What were the consequences of not going through with it? How could I end it? I hadn't thought it through properly and certainly hadn't asked enough questions. I was an idiot, all the things I should have tried to check out beforehand were now obvious. I wondered where that answer machine was, and whether I could find its location and then wipe the message before it was picked up. I knew it wouldn't be possible.

The realisation of the seriousness of the situation I'd got into was becoming greater every minute. I couldn't hand in a letter of resignation; these people would be bad, and I could expect something nasty to happen if I didn't keep up my part of the bargain. I already knew that H liked violence and I suspected that any accomplices he had would be as bad, if not worse. I wondered how long it would be before I received my first job. I needed to mentally prepare myself, but at that moment I didn't feel anywhere near up to it.

I did very little for the rest of the weekend other than sit in my bedroom, worrying about what I'd done. Every time the phone rang, I jumped up nervously thinking it was them. The couple of times my parents called me to the phone saying it was for me. I said, "hello," into the receiver with much trepidation.

My paranoia continued into the next week, and I regularly had the feeling I was being watched. I was jumpy and also as nervous as hell each time I checked my P.O. Box. I did go to the Crooked Billet a couple of times. There was no sign of H there and I wondered if somehow it was connected to me signing up. The only occasions I felt better about the situation was after having a few drinks; the courage alcohol gave me made me feel that I could go through with it. However, the following morning I would revert to my usual fears.

As time passed after the first week, and life continued as usual, my fears started to ease. I was still checking my P.O. box each day, every time a little less concerned about what I'd find. Once a couple of weeks had elapsed after my phone call, my concerns subsided to the point whereby I wondered if it was all just a prank. I hadn't seen H at all during this time to get any confirmation about my call. I started to doubt myself as well; had I phoned the right number? Did I leave my correct address and phone number? I'd been nervous at the time and could have made a mistake. On the other hand, it was unlikely I'd made an error as basic as that and the idea of it being a prank just didn't add up. Why would someone go to such lengths to play a trick like that? Another question I'd failed to ask H was how often jobs came up. After all it can't be a business with a very high or regular turnover. Maybe jobs didn't come up that frequently. Also, I didn't know how many other "employees" were working there. I regularly speculated about the whole affair but came up with no answers. I had nobody to ask, H continuing to be absent from the Crooked Billet.

I began to feel disappointed. In the immediate days after I'd made the call, I was desperate to reverse what I'd done. Now I felt like an opportunity had passed. My life continued as it had before, the same things happening, my general dissatisfaction with it increasing gradually. I began to give up on the idea, thinking somehow something had gone wrong, not knowing how to correct it. I had no way of checking. Even if I rang the number again, I'd only get the answer machine. I scaled down the frequency I went to the post office to check my post to only a couple of times a week. It riled me that I'd probably paid for it for nothing.

Chapter Four

Over five weeks elapsed from the time I'd made the phone call to when I next saw H in the pub. The whole affair was fast beginning to become a distant memory and I hadn't even thought to look over to where H would be, so long had it seemed since I last saw him. I was on my way to the bar when I looked up to see him walking past me towards the door. Before I could react or say anything to him, he was gone. He had glanced at me though and had given me a wink before reaching the door. It stunned me, although I only got a brief glimpse of him. He had a knowing look on his face. It was as though he was trying to be reassuring. I didn't know how to take it, but it did refocus me. I hadn't checked my P.O. Box at the post office for a few days and I decided I would the next day. It made me feel a bit nervous about it again.

The next day I went to the post office for what had become a bit of a routine in opening up my box to find nothing there. This time I was surprised to find a padded envelope. My heart started pounding as soon as I saw it. I looked around, as though expecting to see the person who had sent it watching me. I checked the name and address on the front; perhaps it had been sent to someone else and put in my box by mistake. My name written in print was clearly stated on the front though. I studied the envelope intently. I didn't want to open it there, but I also had to go back to work that afternoon. That would mean not being able to open it until later that evening. I decided I'd have to wait;

it was too risky opening it in public. It felt as though there was quite a bit of paper in it. I thought briefly about opening it in my car when I'd walked back to work. However, I had to start work again shortly, so I just left it in the glove box. It was on my mind the whole afternoon, which dragged like no other.

I had intended to open it in my car as soon as I'd finished work, but I decided to wait a little longer and open in it the security of my bedroom. I was on automatic pilot driving home and wouldn't have been able to recall any of the journey, so much was my mind concentrated on what was in the envelope. It had to be the instructions for my first job, but I wouldn't believe it until I saw it. What would I do? This was a life changing day for me.

I got home and took the envelope straight upstairs to my bedroom. I closed the door and sat on my bed. I studied the envelope once more before taking a deep breath and starting to open it. As I pulled out its contents, the first thing I saw was bank notes, tens and twenties, and lots of them. I'd never seen this much money in my life. The envelope had been stuffed with the money, so much so that I didn't think there was anything else in there at first. Then I noticed a photo. Not a large photo, seemingly standard size when being developed from a camera. In the photo was a woman, probably in her early thirties, smiling naturally, not what seemed a fake smile so often put on by people for the camera. Her face filled almost all the picture, which could have been taken by herself it was so close up. She was subtly good looking. I stared at the photo, I knew there must be something else in the envelope that would give me details, but I also looked at the woman, knowing I'd have to kill her. I wondered what her history was and what she'd done to get herself into a position whereby her photo was now in the hands of someone who was being paid to murder her. I put her photo down and further inspected the contents of the envelope. Aside from the money and the photo, there was one sheet of A4 paper. On it was typed writing. It was nowhere near as detailed as I'd expected or hoped it to be. It gave details of the woman, her name, address and description, which wasn't strictly necessary given the photo was clear enough. Although it did provide height and weight. It stated that the job had no specific deadline to be completed, but that it was to be carried out as soon as possible. Lastly, I read that three thousand pounds had been enclosed, and a further ten thousand would be paid upon successful completion of the contract.

That was it, this was my instruction. H told me that I wouldn't get much assistance, but I'd naively thought I'd get more than basic details. Whilst I had a sickly feeling in my stomach and adrenaline was flowing through me, I didn't feel half as bad as I'd feared I would. Now that I had my first assignment, I could get on with it. After all, there was no going back. Looking back, it was like someone had turned on a switch at that point. I no longer cared about the possible consequences of what I was doing. I'd become the cold, non-caring person I wanted to be. This job certainly matched that personality.

I started counting the money; the notes were used. I wondered if this had come direct from the person who wanted this woman killed. After counting it twice, I'd confirmed to myself that there was exactly three thousand pounds there. This was a huge amount of money to me and to think if I did the job, I'd get another ten thousand. It did occur to me what the going rate for this sort of thing was. How much of a cut did my employers take? They must get a decent proportion. I looked at the typed details again. I noticed the address this time, something I'd not paid attention to when I first read it. She lived far north,

Newcastle. This was a pain, as it meant I'd have to be away for a while. On the positive side though, it would help protect me as once the job was done, I'd be back home miles away. I knew I had to put a plan in place. This was serious work and I had to make sure I was prepared for it.

Over the next couple of days, I spent time organizing myself. I told my boss I would like to have a week off, which he reluctantly agreed to. At first, I was going to pack in my job altogether, especially now I had serious cash behind me, but I thought it would be good to leave the door open just in case. I also thought giving up my job may look suspicious if anything happened and I became a suspect.

I needed a murder weapon. I'd have liked a gun, but obviously these weren't easy to come by. I'd need to think about that for the next time, I was annoyed with myself I hadn't thought about this beforehand. I'd have to settle for a knife instead. I had a good hunting knife from when I went fishing as a teenager. This was good as I didn't want to be seen purchasing one; it would have also been a potential bit of evidence against me were things to go wrong.

I knew I would have to do surveillance on this woman for a while, find out her movements, work out the best time to get her alone and then do the deed. I didn't sleep much over those few days. I was constantly running over a plan in my head, how I'd do it. I was pleased there wasn't a definite deadline. It gave me time to mentally prepare and psyche myself up to go through with it in addition to working out how. The weekend before I headed to Newcastle I tried to act as normal as possible. I went to the Crooked Billet and got drunk with my mates. Notably, H wasn't there. This made me think that seeing him the night before I picked up my package couldn't have been a coincidence. He must have known. He may have been checking to see I was still around.

I told my parents I was going away with some mates for a few days. It was handy that I'd always told them as little as possible about my movements, always being vague when I would be back. This meant I didn't have to constantly advise them if I changed my plans. They had become used to this and therefore questioned me very little on my whereabouts. As long as I gave them a small update of where I was occasionally, they would be happy. I decided that if I returned from Newcastle with the job successfully completed, I'd find my own place, thereby giving me independence and a new life away from any scrutiny. I set off around Monday lunchtime on my mission up north. I felt good, I was doing something positive about my life, moving away from my drab existence. I thought about my ex-girlfriend and the last time I saw her. Doing this would improve my life. It would be exciting in a way that few other people experienced. I thought about my task on the journey. I knew her appearance well. Julie McParland was five feet six inches and weighed nine and a half stone. She had auburn hair, brown eyes and thick lips, probably accentuated by the lipstick she was wearing at the time the photo was taken. There was an air of confidence about her. She was thirty-five years of age. I'd stared at her picture many times over the last few days. What I didn't have any idea of was what her life was like. What she did for a living, did she have a husband, boyfriend or children? Was she well-off or struggling, did she have a car? None of this information had been provided and I needed to find it out if I wanted to carry the job out professionally.

I did have the belief that she was happy in her life, but I was probably influenced in this way because she was smiling in the picture I had of her. It was difficult to imagine her with any other expression.

My first job when I got to Newcastle was to find accommodation. Tempting as it was, with good money in my pocket, to find something decent, I went for basic instead with a cheap chain hotel. I'd bought and studied a map of the area beforehand and found a place in the vicinity of where she lived. I wanted to make sure I got to know nobody whilst I was in Newcastle, as this could give the police a lead at a later date. This meant not even getting friendly with the hotel staff.

Another thing I had to be aware of was that Julie may know that she was in danger. I obviously didn't have a clue what she'd done to have someone pay for her death. I had to assume the worst and that she was permanently on the lookout for somebody like me, who'd been paid good money to bump her off.

Having booked into the hotel, I went to check out where she lived. It was a terraced house on a council estate, not horrible but fairly basic. She hadn't got into her situation by stealing money, that was evident. I decided I'd start my real surveillance the next day. That night I spent time in my hotel room trying to amuse myself watching television on a small screen. I slept fitfully.

I was up early the next morning to start my work. I drove to Julie's road and found a space a little way down from her house. As I waited for her to appear, it struck me that it wouldn't be easy to break into her house, given she lived on a busy road. Although, it would be preferable to do the deed at her home, with the chances of being seen reduced. I left my car briefly to go to a local shop to buy some fags and breakfast. I ate and smoked as I gradually saw the street come to life with more and more residents leaving their homes. There became more space in the street as people drove off to work, unlike the busy road I'd encountered when I'd first arrived. I was getting concerned that either she didn't have a job or I'd missed her leave home when I went to the shop. Soon though, I saw someone leave her house. I strained my eyes to make sure it was her. It certainly looked like the woman in the picture I'd been sent. I was left in little doubt she was my subject. She was dressed in a smart suit and looked business-like. She got into a small, but new car. I started my car, ready to follow her. As I drove past her house to get behind her, I thought how I'd seen nobody else leave her home that morning. This meant that she may live on her own. However, she could still have a husband or boyfriend that left for work later than her. Our journey led further into the city. We drove at a slow pace through the busy traffic. I had to be careful not to lose her.

Around twenty minutes after we'd left her street, she turned into a small car park situated behind a big office block. I struggled to find somewhere to stop; the car park she'd driven into was restricted to card holders only and the road I was on was busy. I stopped illegally a bit further up the road and craned my neck round the headrest. I saw enough to watch her get out of her car and go through a back entrance to the office block. I then continued driving so I could find a proper car park nearby in order to find out more about where she worked on foot. Having done this, I walked around to the front of the building so I could see who it was she worked for. It occurred to me on the way that there weren't many parking spaces in the car park she'd driven into compared with the size of the office block. This meant that either most staff parked somewhere else or she was privileged to have a space. It could be that she was senior or had good connections. I noted that the company Julie worked for was an insurance company. In my short experience of following her, her life seemed very normal and routine. There was nothing to suggest she was the sort of person upsetting people to the point they wanted her dead. I hung around town for most of the day, occasionally looking to see if her car was still in the car park. Later in the day, just before five, I waited outside her office, trying to be as subtle as possible. I knew that I wouldn't be able to wait in my car outside the car park and so decided I'd stay on foot, watch her come out and then make sure she got in her car. I'd then get mine and drive to her house to see if she'd gone home. I'd also be able see if anyone else left work with her. I half expected something sinister to happen, but nothing did. I was caught up in the idea that she was somehow involved in something dodgy, even though there was nothing unusual in her actions so far.

I waited outside her office. Just before five thirty, she appeared. She got into her car and drove off alone. I retrieved my car and drove back to where she lived. Her car was parked outside. It really hit me then. How the hell was I going to kill her? I didn't have a clue. I had a dangerous knife, but I could hardly accost her coming out of her home or work without expecting many witnesses and a real struggle. I had to get her on her own, and that meant either catching her in a public place out of view, which was unlikely, or somehow gaining access to her home. This had potential, I thought. Firstly, I had to make sure she did live on her own. I stayed, bored out of my head, watching her house all evening. Sure enough, there was no movement in terms of anyone leaving or arriving. I hadn't realised how drab a job like this could be. I thought it would be exciting, but I'd just had the most boring day of my life. As I drove back to my hotel, I began to think of ways I could break into her home. I'd at least been successful in ascertaining that she probably lived on her own, so I could take some comfort in that I'd achieved something. My options as far as I could see were either breaking into her home directly, getting access through posing as someone with fake identity or somehow gaining her trust so she'd invite me in. Breaking in seemed a good idea; I knew she was out all day so I could pick my moment and then lie in wait for her. However, the house wasn't easily accessible, especially as it didn't have side access, being terraced. In addition, there always seemed to be people about on the road. The second option of posing as someone seemed plausible. If I could get a foot in the door then I'd be in with a good chance of quickly overpowering her. But I would need to be very quick and there was a big risk she would manage to force the door shut before I could get in or maybe alert passers-by The last option of gaining her trust appealed to me, but wasn't really plausible and was fraught with danger. I went to sleep that night, none the wiser as to how I was going to complete my task.

    The next few days I settled into a routine of following her. It was as boring as could be and I learned little or nothing about her. She went to work for roughly the same hours every day and then went home. One night she went out in her car. I followed her to a pizza restaurant where she met a friend and had dinner for a couple of hours before returning home for the evening. Nothing untoward happened; her life was almost too normal and routine to be true. I was getting more and more desperate. I still hadn't developed any ideas of when I was going to kill her, and I could see no easy way to get close to her to open up an opportunity for myself. I knew, despite my concerns I couldn't be rash. One stupid move and I could end any chance I had.

    My hopes drifted towards the weekend. She might venture out without her car and potentially an opportunity to get her on her own in a sheltered area might arise. However, I realised there was a touch of false optimism to these thoughts. Sure enough though, on Friday night, she left her home on foot, leaving her car in her street. I followed her, also on foot. She caught a bus into the town centre and went into a bar. I hoped she hadn't noticed me in tow along the way. In the bar she met a group of people. There were about six of them, which was disconcerting. If I was going to get to know her, the fewer people around her the better. I kept my distance and stayed over the other side of the bar. Apart from the odd beer to kill time in the week, I'd had little to drink since I'd been up north. I enjoyed having a few beers, although having them on my own as well as deliberately not talking to anyone was difficult. The bars seemed friendlier than down south and I was sure that should I want to strike up a conversation with the locals, I'd be welcome. I was in there for a couple of hours before Julie and her friends moved on. I followed them out of the bar. I worried that I was carrying out a fruitless exercise and that no opportunity would arise to carry out the killing. I felt low and concerned about the whole affair. What if I didn't get the chance or couldn't do it? What would happen to me? I also couldn't be up here forever.

    I followed Julie and her friends across the city for about ten minutes. Fortunately, the night was busy, which it made it easier for me to look inconspicuous tracking them. As I feared they would, they went towards what looked like a nightclub. I don't know where I was hoping they'd end up, but it wasn't in one of these places. I watched them join the back of a small queue. On the door were three big, mean-looking bouncers, typical of such an establishment. There was no way I could follow Julie's group in. I may get searched and, given I had a large hunting knife strapped to my leg, this wasn't a good idea. I thought that being on my own would only increase the likelihood of me being searched. I also didn't like the idea of being in a club on my own. I'd stick out like a sore thumb. It was one thing being in a pub or a bar alone, but in a club, it looked strange, and I knew this would make me feel uncomfortable. I was tempted to throw in the towel and go back to my hotel for the evening. However, in the back of my mind, I knew there was perhaps a small chance I could get at her later. I didn't want to miss the possibility, even though at that point I didn't feel very hopeful. She'd probably be drunk if I did catch her coming out of the club which would be to my advantage.

Waiting in a city full of drunkards, some looking for trouble, others loud and abusive, the occasional person being sick from too much alcohol was far from pleasant. It made me realise what a tough job the police had and why our city culture was frowned upon by many people. I'd never really seen it from the other side, always being one who was drunk if out at this time of night.

I knew I could be hanging around for a couple of hours, so I went to get something to eat, in a greasy burger establishment, just to pass the time more than anything else. Waiting around outside the club made me feel uneasy. I was sure the police looked at me with suspicion on a couple of occasions which didn't bode well. I was also paranoid I'd miss her coming out of the club. If she left at closing time, it would be easy to do so, considering these types of places could hold hundreds of people.

However, I was pleased to see her exit the club around half an hour before it was due to close. The bad news was that she was with a guy. He was not part of the original group she went there with earlier. I could see she was giggling and acting inebriated. Chances were, they were going back to one of their places and I would have just wasted another evening no nearer to completing my aim. They got into a cab at a taxi rank a few hundred metres away from the club. I quickly jumped into the cab behind them and barked the corny line of "follow that cab," at the driver. He eyed me with intrigue, as though wondering what my game was. It wasn't long before his curiosity got the better of him and he asked me why I wanted to follow the people in front of me. It was a reasonable question, as the only time I'd done this before had been when there were too many of people in my group to fit into one cab. I told him it was a long story and left it that, hoping he'd realise it was none of his business. The cabbie did not hide his disappointment at me not divulging further information. I imagined him speculating the situation.

I wasn't happy as I was now opening myself up to witnesses, what with standing outside the club for a while and then talking to the cab driver. There was more than a strong likelihood that I'd be on some CCTV footage around the city as well. Therefore, there'd be plenty of leads for the police should I carry out my task tonight. However, that was looking increasingly unlikely. From my new knowledge of the geography of the city we seemed to be heading towards Julie's home. I wondered if she knew the guy in the cab with her prior to tonight or had just pulled him in the club. She didn't hang about if she did, and this was maybe the first sign that she wasn't squeaky clean, although hardly a crime or unusual. But it made me think that it could maybe be an ex who wanted her dead. Perhaps she had carried on playing the field whilst in a relationship, or it could be another girl who'd found out she'd been having an affair with her man.

Although, in my opinion, neither of these possibilities warranted killing someone. I thought about whether if I'd found out my ex-girlfriend had gone behind my back, what action I would have taken. It would have annoyed me, no doubt, and the thought of giving the guy a good kicking and my girlfriend a real mouthful would have occurred to me, but I wouldn't have dreamed as going as far as having someone killed over it. I wondered whether she was seeing anybody when we split up. Even though I had no real reason to suspect it, I'd thought regularly that it may be the case since we parted. It would have explained her ending the relationship in what to me was an out of the blue manner. She'd possibly found someone she thought was better. After all, despite my feelings, we hardly acted head over heels in love. Our relationship had always remained casual, in that we only saw each other a couple of times a week and never spoke about what we'd do long term, or if we'd ever move in together.

The car slowed down and I looked around, not recognising where we were at first. The taxi Julie and her friend were in had pulled over and I was puzzled as to what was going on. Getting my bearings, I realised that we had stopped just a few streets from Julie's house. Maybe this was where the guy lived, and they were just innocently sharing a cab home as they lived near each other. My taxi had pulled in right behind them, which I didn't want to happen. However, I'd been too slow communicating this to the driver. Julie and her accomplice had both stepped out the car, crushing my theory of them sharing a cab to their respective homes and were standing on the pavement talking. I settled the tab with the driver of my cab and got out. I immediately turned away from the couple and walked away at a brisk pace. It would possibly appear strange to them that another cab had pulled up directly behind theirs and I didn't want them catching a good glimpse of me.

As I walked the first few steps away from where they were, I heard them talking in raised voices, possibly arguing. Frustratingly, I couldn't catch many of their words to distinguish the subject of their discussion but there was tension in their voices. I was tempted to hang around to listen to what they were saying but I knew this would just attract attention. I carried on walking away. About a hundred metres away from where they were standing there was a junction with a road leading off to the right. I turned down the road and stopped just out of sight of where they were. I hoped that they'd been significantly engrossed in their argument not to have noticed me. I stayed where I was and tried to listen for them, but despite it being quiet I couldn't make out their voices. There was nobody else around, which was good. I peered back around the corner I'd just turned down, looking around somebody's hedge to do so. The houses on the road I stood in were marginally nicer, in that they had small front gardens rather than doors that opened directly onto the street. I was crouched down and I could see Julie and the guy still talking. They looked more animated now and I assumed that their argument had heated up further. Occasionally, I thought I could make out raised voices, but I wasn't sure if I was just imagining this. I wondered what they were arguing about. They must have known each other prior to tonight. It was unlikely they met tonight, decided to leave together and were then arguing before they had reached home. I wished I knew more about Julie's life, but I supposed that not knowing made my task easier from the point of view I had no connection to her and also cared less what happened to her.

I looked away from where they were and sat down with my back to the hedge. I stared up at the windows of the houses around me. One or two had lights on but the majority were in darkness and I could see nobody peering out of them. I knew I'd make a very suspicious character to anyone who did spot me. I peered back around the hedge again. As I did so, I saw the man who Julie had been talking to heading in my direction. He was walking purposefully and appeared annoyed. I could just make out Julie walking in the other direction. I looked around and saw a large four by four parked across the road. I'd have to hide behind that whilst the guy walked past. Hopefully he wouldn't see me. I ran over to it and positioned myself the other side of the car, crouched down low out of site. I then got down on all fours to see if I could watch him coming past from under the car. The angle wasn't very good so I couldn't see beyond the car very far. However, within a matter of seconds, I heard him coming. Because it was quiet, I could make out his footsteps. I also heard him mumbling to himself. As he got nearer it sounded like he was cursing. I imagined he was drunk as well as angry. I could now just about see his feet from my view under the car and I could make out that he was carrying straight on rather than turning into the road I was in. As he went past the road, I timed it so that I made my way quietly round the back of the car as he walked past to remain obscured from him.

I waited for a few seconds for him to get further away before I walked back towards the direction he'd come from. As I got to the corner, I could see him trudging further up the road; hopefully he wouldn't turn around and see me. I could see no sign of Julie as I walked back to where I'd got out of the taxi. I broke into a run knowing she'd have walked off in the direction away from me. I knew roughly where she lived but I had to think quickly of the fastest route to get there from where I was. Working it through my head, I realised it wasn't far, and I kept running in the hope I'd catch up with her.

I got to her road within a couple of minutes, but I was worried I wasn't going to get there before she got inside her home. My luck was in. I looked up her road to see that she was still within a short distance of her house. I was out of breath; I was less fit than I realised. I hadn't run that far for so long. This was another thing I needed to do if I wanted to stay in this game. Take better care of myself and exercise regularly. I still had to continue running though, as if I didn't, she'd be inside before I got there. I was trying not to make too much noise so she wouldn't notice me approaching, which wasn't easy. It was still and quiet around so as I neared her, I knew it was likely she'd hear me.

By this stage Julie was outside her house and I was only a short distance away. She was looking in her bag. It gave me time to slow down to walking pace and be more discreet in my approach. It took her a few seconds to locate her keys. She was now putting them in the door, I was only a few metres away and had slowed right down. Suddenly, and much later than I'd anticipated, she became aware of my presence. She turned her head sharply in my direction, one hand on the key that was in the lock, the other gripping her handbag. I looked straight back at her. This was the closest I'd been to her. Her expression of initial surprise of seeing someone so close turned very quickly to one of fear. It was almost as if she knew why I was there. I could see panic go right through her. I wanted her to unlock the door so I could force her inside. I couldn't do it on the street. As she managed, with frantic hands to open the door, I arrived next to her. The timing was perfect. I gave her a big shove in through her doorway. The door slammed against the wall. She stumbled backwards, but I had to give her another push before I could get in the house far enough to be able to shut the door. The second push made her fall to the ground, and as she did, she gave a yelp. It was like the sound a dog makes when its tail had just been stood on. She was shaking and breathless. I slammed the door shut. She tried to get up as I did this, but I turned around quickly enough to push her back to the floor. I knelt on top of her to pin her to the floor and at the same time tried to get my knife out from the strapping on my leg. She was now becoming frantic, screaming, kicking and punching me. Her punches were weak and harmless. She was in such a state of panic they weren't accurate or effective. I wanted to stop her screaming so I had one hand trying to get the knife whilst the other was trying to cover her mouth. I finally got hold of my knife, and within seconds I'd plunged it into her body. She let out a huge scream, a different type to that of the others she'd been emitting.

It was now my turn to panic and I pulled the knife back out and started to stab her continuously. Her screaming continued; it was now like that of a dying animal you hear on nature programmes when caught by its predator. Desperate to stop the noise and before I knew what I was really doing, I plunged the knife into her head. Everything went quiet. I turned away from Julie's now limp body. I felt physically sick. I couldn't believe I'd done it. I sat with my back to the wall for a few seconds, drawing in breaths of air, trying to calm down. I wanted to shut down and just sleep there and then, but I knew I had to think clearly to make sure I got out of there without leaving too much evidence, as well as before anybody who may have heard her screams arrived. When I thought about the situation I was in, I was overcome with fear. It felt desperate. I managed to get my mind calm for a few seconds and stood to assess the scene. I could hear nothing outside or any movement from the neighbours. I looked at the body, something I'd rather not do. It was squirmed up in an unusual way and there was a look of horror on her face, unsurprisingly. Seeing her brought home to me once more the seriousness of the crime I'd committed. I'd just taken a life, barbarically. A great temptation came over me to escape the scene as quickly as possible. I felt like running until I could run no more. Instead, I took a deep breath. First, I had to get the knife out. The fact that it was buried deep in the side of her head made the prospect of this very uninviting. I knew the more I thought about it, the harder it would be to do, so I counted to three, bent down and grabbed it hard in one movement. I could barely look to see what remnants there were of the inside of Julie's head on the knife. Once again, I had the urge to be sick. This was quickly replaced with my original desire to be out of there.

I thought about the events that took place since I had got into the house, the only things I'd touched, as far as I could remember, were the door and Julie. I had a tissue stuffed in my pocket; I took it out and wiped in a big area around where I'd thought I'd shut the door. I looked at Julie, I'd touched her many times during our scuffle. Could you take fingerprints from people's clothing or material? I didn't know for certain. There didn't seem much I could do about it anyway and fortunately the police didn't have mine, so it could only come back to me should they trace me through some other evidence. I certainly wasn't going to take the time to remove her clothes and take them with me. Although, afterwards I wondered if I should have, as the motive for her killing may have been mistaken as a failed rape attempt.

I looked down at myself; there was quite a bit of blood on me. I had to get back to my hotel without being seen by anyone. I placed the knife in my sock under my jeans. I opened the door using the tissue to prevent getting further fingerprints on the handle. I stepped outside and pulled the door shut firmly behind me. I looked around; it was still quiet, fortunately. I took a deep breath and walked swiftly to my car.

Driving back to my hotel was like an out of body experience.

It was as though I was someone else and that what had just happened wasn't reality. I wondered a couple of times whether I was dreaming and if I could verify this somehow. I then thought that if it was a dream, the severity of the nightmare I was having would have woken me by this stage.

I got back to my hotel and went straight to bed, marginally buoyed by not bumping into anyone on my way from the hotel car park. Against my expectations, I fell asleep quickly and slept well. I wondered afterwards if this was a reaction to the shock of my experiences that night.

I woke up well into the next morning. I knew I'd been dreaming, and that my dreams were intense, but I couldn't remember what they were about. Replaying the events of last night brought a range of emotions to me. For the first time since I'd done it, I congratulated myself on carrying out the murder. I'd doubted whether I was capable of doing it as well as whether I'd get a decent opportunity, but I'd achieved what I'd set out to do. I also thought about the cash this would bring me. I'd be rich by my standards. However, these thoughts were countered by the fact that I'd killed someone in cold blood and would most likely be given a life sentence in prison if caught. This was a terrifying prospect and, naively, one I hadn't given a huge amount of thought to before now.

Soon after I'd woken up that morning, my paranoia began. Any unusual noise startled me and had me wondering if the police were coming for me. As I lay in my hotel room, I thought I could hear knocking on the door. I constantly peered through the spy hole to see if anyone was waiting outside. I didn't want to leave my room that day. I got through all the fags I had on me.

When I was composed, I thought through my next steps and what I needed to do before I headed home. The temptation was to get back down south and out of there as soon as possible. However, despite this urge, I didn't want it to coincide with the murder. If I stayed a couple of more days, I thought my departure time would look less suspicious. I also had to work out what I was going to do with my blood-stained clothes and the knife. These items were major evidence and I had to get shot of them safely and quickly. I didn't want to get rid of them in Newcastle, as to me it seemed more likely they'd be found there during police investigations. I decided I'd dispose of them somewhere on my way back down south. In the meantime, I'd have to take a big risk and keep them in my room or my car.

I eventually went out late afternoon to get something to eat and buy more cigarettes. It was a Saturday and, although life continued as normal, the world suddenly seemed a different place. People treated me in the same way, but I'd somehow expected them to react differently, as though they knew what I'd done. I saw the police a couple of times which sent me into a panic. No matter how much I tried to stay calm, I couldn't.

I returned to the safety of my hotel room, armed with the cigarettes and food I'd purchased to get me through the rest of the day. The evening passed painfully slow and my paranoia didn't subside, if anything increasing. I continued to be jumpy at the sound of noises outside and regularly looked through the spy hole in the hotel door.

Later when it was time to sleep, things didn't get better. Whereas the previous night I slept well, this night was the opposite. I was tossing and turning and images of Julie's face after I'd killed her kept flicking into my head. I was constantly replaying the whole incident and wondering if anyone had seen me. I thought about whether she'd been found yet and what sort of investigations the police were doing; had they found any evidence to put me in the frame? There was also the guy Julie had had the argument with. He would have seen me at some point getting out of the taxi behind him and Julie. I thought about whether he'd been consciously aware of my presence. On the positive side for me though, he would also be in the frame in the eyes of the police. Julie's friends were likely to know he'd left the club with her and the taxi driver could verify this too. This was something to cling onto. The fact that an innocent person could be put in prison for what I'd done didn't bother me at all. I truly had to look after myself now and no one else.

The next day was extremely boring and uneventful which I regarded as a good thing. I resisted the temptation to bail early and start home. My paranoia continued and I spent another day on edge. I did manage to go out once, my cabin fever forcing me to leave the hotel for some fresh air, a short walk and some food, even though I wasn't hungry. I didn't want to buy a paper. I wanted to avoid any possible media attention on the crime I'd committed. I assumed it would be a big enough story to make local or even national news when it was uncovered. I had also avoided watching the news on the television in my room.

It was a relief when Monday morning arrived. I'd had another restless night and I was beginning to know what insomnia felt like. I settled my hotel bill and started my way down south. It had been a week since I arrived in Newcastle, but it had felt like a lifetime. My life had certainly changed dramatically in the time I was there.

After driving for about an hour, I pulled off the A1 and found a town. I had some shopping to do. I bought a spade, some tape, a couple of dust bags, a paper weight and a bottle of meths. Moving further on I drove for a while longer before heading off the main road again. I wanted to find some isolated woodland

and I had to search for a while to find the perfect spot. The woodland was dense and quiet. Drenching my blood-stained clothes with the meths I set fire to them. They burned quickly, too quickly and I struggled to keep the fire under control. Fortunately, I was eventually helped by the sodden ground.

Once they'd burned away, I shovelled their ashen remains into one of the bags. I found another quieter spot and was once again favoured by the wet ground; this time it allowed me to dig a reasonable size hole to bury the bag. The next thing to do deal with was the knife.

Back in the car I covered further distance before stopping again for this last job. This time I needed to find water. I'd planned to stop by a river that I'd seen on the map. I parked the car and looked around me to see if many people were about. I had to wait a while before it was clear, and when it was, I opened the bag that I had kept in the foot well of the passenger side of the car. I took out the knife and also the paperweight and sticky tape that I'd bought earlier. I wrapped the tape around the knife and paperweight so they were tied together and then further wrapped one of the plastic bags around them, securing them with plenty more tape. I was parked on a road that ran alongside the river. There was a grass verge in between the two. I got out the car with my package and waited for the immediate area to be quiet. I wanted to get a good throw in so that the knife splashed into the middle of the river where it'd be at its deepest. I gave myself the all clear and achieved my goal with a direct throw. It felt like my work was done.

My paranoia continued as I made my final leg of the journey home. Certain cars that stayed behind me, irrespective of what lane I chose to drive in, made me think that unmarked police cars were following me. It also got me thinking that my car could be major evidence against me. After all, I'd been sat in it in Julie's road for quite a lot of the week prior to her death and it had also been there the night of the murder. Someone in her road may have spotted this and reported it once the police started any investigation. I could get rid of it, but that wouldn't make much difference, as I'd still be the registered owner at the time of the crime. There was nothing I could do except hope the residents in Julie's road were not that observant. Another thing I didn't feel comfortable about was having a spade and a bottle of partially used meths in my car: not a crime in itself, but would take some explaining if I was stopped. It was driving me mad, the constant thinking about what could incriminate me and whether the police were on to me.

Chapter Five

Back in London, I stopped near home. I needed to buy more fags. The last week had not helped me cut down on smoking. I dumped the meths in a street bin. I'd bought the spade from a chain store, one of which was not too far from where I lived. I thought I'd take it back, but then I thought it would look strange, having only purchased it a few hours earlier that day in a northern store. I'd need to think that one over and, in the meantime, it could remain in the boot of my car.

Back home, I had some explaining to do, which I certainly wasn't in the mood for. I hadn't spoken to my parents the whole time I was in Newcastle. They were expecting me to be away for a few days, not a whole week, so much lying had to be done. This only made me want to move in on my own even more. As well as providing explanations of my whereabouts to my parents, I also had to phone my boss and make excuses as to where I'd been. He wouldn't be happy with me either, as he'd expected me back at work that Monday morning. Lying became easier and easier though and a regular part of my life. For me to survive, I had to hone this skill. With my parents and my boss both appeased for now, my life returned to some sort of normality. This helped a little to allay my fear of the possible consequences that faced me for what I'd done.

Nothing out of the ordinary happened over the next ten days. I did get a few questions from my mates as to where I'd been the previous week; it was unusual for me not to make an appearance at the Crooked Billet at least once or twice during a weekend. They were easily fobbed off with a story about me being away with a couple of work mates. During this period, my poor sleeping pattern and paranoia continued, but as each day passed and I received no visit from the police, I felt like I'd taken another small step to safety.

One thing I did realise in the first week and a half after my return from Newcastle was how much I detested my day job. I wanted to stay in it, not just to appear to be continuing life normally, but also because, until I got a few jobs under my belt in the new line of work I had, I didn't have enough money to feel secure. However, the thought of having enough money to give up my building work didn't stop me having severe doubts about the path I'd chosen. The experience of Newcastle hardened me, but I found it difficult not to be able to tell anyone about it. It wasn't just that I wanted to share my problems and fears with another person, it would have just been good to be able to relay my story to someone. In some ways it was impressive I'd achieved my goal, and to be able to tell someone would have perhaps made me feel better. Another thing would be to discuss what I did right or wrong. In any other job you get feedback on your performance and on the job tuition. For this, I was left completely to my own devices. Still, in other ways, having a secret life that nobody knew about also made me feel superior. I enjoyed that fact that people didn't know the real me.

Ten days after I'd arrived back in London, I visited my P.O. Box. I had already been a couple of times and was beginning to wonder whether I'd get my completion payment. It did occur to me that I'd been stitched up and what I'd done was just a scam by H to get Julie killed. However, that day I opened my box to find a large envelope. I waited until I got home before I opened it. I already had a good idea as to what it was. It felt like what I'd been waiting for and I wasn't disappointed. The envelope was crammed with notes: exactly ten thousand pounds, as I'd been promised. I couldn't believe they'd sent this sort of cash through the post. Although, I suppose for whoever sent it, it was risk free. There was little to trace the sender from. My name and P.O. Box address was typed on the front of the letter and it had probably been wiped free of fingerprints or handled with gloves. If the envelope had been intercepted, all the questions would have been mine to face, and what did I know about the whole operation other than my acquaintance with H, who had disappeared.

I was delighted with the amount of cash I'd earned. It was far more money than I'd ever had and would have taken me ages to earn that much in the building game. The only problem I had was what to do with it. I didn't want to pay it into the bank. Not only would that be incriminating, I could even get tax queries about it. And I wasn't happy with my short-term solution of hiding it in my bedroom either. It was too much money to risk losing through a burglary. It was something else I needed to think about; again, it would have been nice to consult someone and get advice on. Money laundering wasn't something you could just casually ask about.

Over the next month, my life got better, my paranoia, fears and occasional nightmares subsided, and with each passing day, I genuinely believed I'd got away with it. With the extra cash, I could enjoy my life to the full, and by the end of the month, I'd found a local flat and moved in. It was great to have my own place and the feeling of independence. My efforts in Newcastle had come with some reward. H was still noticeably absent from the Crooked Billet. I wanted to ask people in there if they knew his whereabouts, but realised this wasn't a good idea, as linking him with me might push me into the hands of the police at a later date.

I had managed to stick at my job, which I was becoming more and more unhappy with. If I was assigned another job, that might allow me to chuck it in. Although, of course I had no way of knowing whether this would be the case. There was no way of predicting it. I just had to wait and see.

One night out during this time I did bump into my ex-girlfriend again. It was in a club me and my mates had gone onto after a few drinks in the Crooked Billet. She was in there with a couple of friends and was happy to come over and talk to me. I remember she annoyed me because she talked to me as though nothing had ever happened between us. She also mentioned she'd got a new boyfriend, which didn't help matters. I was quite short with her, fuelled by alcohol, and pretty much told her I was doing better since we'd parted; I could see this annoyed her, so I walked off before she could get a retort in. I spent a lot of the remainder of the evening watching her. She was on the dance floor a lot and seemingly having a good time. I dare not admit it to myself, but I still wasn't over her. It was watching her more than ever that made me want to tell someone about what I'd done. Even though she wouldn't have remotely approved, it would have been great to tell her. She was the only person I felt close enough to. However, we were no longer a couple, so it wasn't possible. The next morning, I regretted the way I'd spoken to her and realised I'd acted childishly. I was tempted to ring her to apologise but felt it was best left alone. I had to forget about her.

The only thing I'd done towards my new line of work since my first job, had been to call the number I'd been given by H and leave a message with my new phone number of the flat I'd moved into. I'd given it some thought beforehand and came to the conclusion that if they did ring home and my parents told them I'd moved out, they might get the idea that I'd done a runner after my first job and was severing ties. So, although part of me wasn't sure I wanted to be encouraging work, I thought it was best I was upfront with them. I still didn't know and didn't like to think about the consequences of walking away from it all.

I'd given plenty of thought to what new line of daytime work I could do to get away from the building trade. I struggled to think of anything suitable that I could turn my hand to and in the back of my mind was the idea of giving up work altogether. If I had a couple of more assassin jobs behind me, it would be possible. However, I knew this would be difficult from the point of view of explaining to friends and family where I got my money from. Already one or two of my mates had commented that I seemed to have more money than I used to have.

One evening a couple of weeks after moving into my new place, my phone rang. When I answered, I received a rather muffled message telling me to check my P.O. Box the next day. It set my pulse rate sky high immediately. I was going to have to kill someone again. Although I'd known this was likely to happen, being told for definite was still shocking. Part of me wanted to continue after my first success, but on the other hand, I'd seemingly got away with my first assassination and knew I might not be so lucky the next time.

As soon as the person at the other end of the phone finished the message, they hung up. It was definitely a man, but other than that I couldn't form any other characteristics about the person, such as accent or age. I guessed they were talking through something that distorted their voice. I checked immediately after the call had ended what number had called me, but, as I knew would be the case, the caller had withheld the number. Who were these people? How many of them controlled the operation and from where? How did they attract business? After all, they could hardly advertise. I was also wondering how many people like me there were, people who received assignments to do their dirty work.

The next day, I did as I was told and went to the post office. Sure enough, inside my box was an envelope. Mission number two had arrived. My feelings were a mixture of excitement and fear. I wondered where I'd be off to this time.

Once again, I waited until I was home before opening the envelope. The system wasn't much different from last time. However, the target was a man in his forties. He lived in Neath in Wales. He looked like an ordinary middle-aged man, with slightly greying hair and glasses. I would barely notice him on the street. He was a reasonable size though, described as five feet eleven in height in the few details I was provided with. It went through my mind that he would not be easy to overpower. From that point of view, Julie had been a simpler first hit, in that I'd been able to pin her down relatively easily. This guy, called Paul Donaldson, would be a different prospect. I knew I'd have to change my strategy and I did have an idea about it.

On the positive side, he was worth more money. I'd received four thousand pounds up front and would get a further twelve upon completion. I wondered if there were standard rates and because he was stronger and seemingly more athletic, he attracted a higher fee. Could it be as simple as that, or were negotiations carried out and a price was agreed upon between client and service provider? It was as much as a mystery to me as everything else in this affair.

Once again, there wasn't a strict deadline imposed on me to carry out my killing. This was a big positive for me, as I felt I needed time to get myself organised. The first thing I had to do was to speak to one of my mates. I'd been talking to him a couple of weeks earlier and he'd mentioned he knew someone who could get guns. I can't remember why he even brought it up, but I was immediately interested. I didn't want to appear overly keen, as I didn't want him thinking I wanted one for myself. I managed to casually carry on the conversation enough though to find out that it was possible to get in touch with this guy and buy one.

Sitting on my bed looking at the details of my latest assignment, I knew I had to persuade my mate to give me the number of his contact who dealt firearms. This wouldn't be easy given that I, of course, couldn't remotely tell him the real reason why I wanted to purchase a gun.

I waited until the weekend when I'd be able to see him in the Billet. I didn't want to contact him directly beforehand, as I suspected this would have only fuelled his suspicions. Annoyingly, he wasn't there on Friday and I had to wait until Saturday before I saw him.

As soon as we said hello, I just came right out and asked him for this guy's number. Immediately, he responded, "Please tell me it's not for you."

"No, it's not. It's a long story, but it's for a mate," I said, lying. I thought I sounded convincing. I was honing a good skill in concealing the truth.

"I've got the time to listen to it," Brad replied.

I'd known Brad since school and he was the sort of mate who'd do anything for you. A real salt of the earth. He was probably one of the most caring mates I had. Ironically, he was one of the last mates I had who I'd suspect of knowing someone who sold guns on the black market. However, he knew some dodgy people from his job. He worked in marketing for a nightclub company and had got to know some of the bouncers. I suspected this was where his contact came from.

"Look mate, I'd love to tell you more, but I've got to keep it quiet. All I can tell you is a good friend is in a bit of trouble and he needs a bit of security."

"Anyone I know?" Brad asked.

"No, mate."

Brad looked pensive. I could tell he wanted to say no, but he also didn't want to miss the chance of doing a mate a favour, even if it was a dodgy one.

"All right," he said with a large sigh. "But I hope you know what you're doing."

"You can trust me," I lied.

We got a pen and paper from the bar and he gave me the number of his contact. No more was said on the matter.

I phoned the guy, called Jason, the next Monday. It didn't feel right to disturb his weekend, and I didn't want to annoy him. The voice that answered the phone was exactly how I imagined it to be, a deep, heavy London accent and abrupt. I told him I wanted to buy something from him, leaving the specifics out for now. He asked me many questions. Who was I? How did I get his number? Where did I know Brad from? How long I'd know him? He was paranoid and gave the clear impression he didn't trust anyone. Once I'd answered all his questions, he suggested a meeting time. He told me the name of a pub he drank in and that he'd be there on Wednesday night.

I was unsurprisingly nervous going to the pub that night. I thought this guy would probably be a big time criminal. I'd realised after our call on Monday that I didn't have a clue what he looked like. I could hardly go around the pub asking people if their name was Jason, and did they sell guns because I was there to buy one. So, after weighing up my options, I phoned Brad. I didn't fancy ringing Jason back to ask him to describe himself, it would somehow seem amateurish.

Brad and I talked about our weekend before I asked him the question as casually as I could.

"Are you sure about this, mate?" he replied.

"Yes," I responded. "My mate is going to meet him. He just needs to know what he looks like," I lied, knowing if I told Brad I was meeting him directly this would seriously concern him.

It was clear from his tone that Brad was still uncomfortable with the whole situation, but having already given me Jason's details, he didn't have much of a choice but to give me the information I needed and started describing Jason. He was in his early twenties, about six feet, well built, with a shaved head and had a distinguishing feature that I'd recognise him by. His left hand was like a claw rather than a hand, as he'd lost three fingers when he was younger.

"Don't ever ask him about it though. He hates talking about it," Brad told me.

"Do you know how it happened?" I asked.

"No, but the one time I did hear someone mention it, it almost got very nasty."

"Oh, I'll tell my mate not to say a word then."

I stood outside the pub Jason had told me to meet him in. The White Horse didn't look the most welcoming of pubs. A rusty old sign, with a faded picture of a white horse that was only just distinguishable, swung gently in the breeze. The pub looked in much need of a makeover. In addition, the area it stood in was well known as being run down. It was nine o'clock, the time I'd targeted to be there. I hadn't wanted to arrive earlier as I wasn't sure what time Jason would get there. On the other hand, I didn't want to get there much later, as I thought it might be worse to speak to him when he was more likely to be drunk.

There weren't too many people in the pub, and I had a clear path to the bar. I bought a pint from a stroppy bar maid who did nothing to enhance the image of the place and scanned my surroundings. I knew that, for whatever reason, I'd feel more comfortable approaching Jason with a beer in my hand. At the bar around the other side of the pub were a group of people who looked like they might be Jason's crowd. Some of them were playing pool, the others standing watching or talking. I waited for a couple of minutes, looking discreetly at them. They seemed a big group. There were girls amongst them, but mainly it consisted of blokes. There were a couple of them potentially matching the description I'd been given. Studying them further, I thought I could see who I believed to be Jason standing at the bar with a couple of people. I couldn't really see his hands well from my position to verify my hunch though. I'd have to go over there and find out. I took a big gulp of my beer and walked towards them, my heartbeat increasing with each step I took. I felt very nervous.

As I got nearer, I saw my initial inkling was right. The guy who I'd assumed to be Jason did indeed have a deformed left hand. He was standing with two other people, a guy who was also well built and a very good-looking girl. I was temporarily stunned by her. She was amazingly beautiful, almost like no other girl I'd seen. I consciously made an effort to take my eyes off her and I nudged my way gingerly into the group. All three of them stared at me as I did this, although they continued talking as I stood there.

"Are you Jason?" I asked, interrupting them.

"Yeah. Why?" He responded, immediately aggressive and showing annoyance that I'd stopped them in mid-conversation. I introduced myself and held out my hand to shake. Jason didn't move. He stared at me with a look of confusion on his face; he obviously didn't remember me or why I was there.

"I phoned you the other night. I'm a mate of Brad's."

For a couple of seconds even this didn't clarify it, but suddenly it clicked.

"Oh, yeah," he said. "What do you want?"

I wasn't expecting him to be so direct, but he obviously didn't care for pleasantries. I looked at him, his mate and the good-looking girl. They were all staring back at me. I was expecting that we'd have a quiet chat in the corner of the pub somewhere, not that he'd get me to talk about it here in the open, in front of people. I whispered the words, "A gun."

"What?" he questioned, starting to look exasperated that I was taking up his precious time.

"A gun," I repeated a little louder, still barely more audible than a whisper. As I finished, I quickly looked around to see if anyone had heard what I said other than the three people I was talking to. When I looked back towards Jason; I saw he was grinning. He had very white teeth, the sort a toothpaste company would use in an advert.

"Really?" he said mockingly. I glanced at the other two. His mate and the girl were also grinning at me. If only I had a girlfriend like that, I thought, as I eyed her. She was perfection.

"Yes," I replied trying to look and sound serious.

I was trying my best not to stare at his deformed hand or at the girl. This, I didn't find easy.

"You're out of your league, mate," he said. I was now starting to feel very small in addition to feeling intimidated. He was starting to humiliate me, and in front of the girl as well. Although I was distracted by the conversation, the more I looked at her, the more I was struck by her beauty. Her individual features were not necessarily striking, standard brown eyes, a nose marginally on the small side, and lips not excessively thick, but somehow when put together it worked.

"I'm not out of my league, I'm deadly serious," I responded.

He sneered and mimicked my voice, "I'm deadly serious," showing he wasn't impressed by my presence or request. "OK. What you going to do with it, bro?"

I was worried he'd asked me this and I wasn't sure how to respond. I certainly wasn't going to tell him the truth. So that left me with the options of either lying or somehow dodging the question. I took a sip of my beer, trying to retain my cool. I kept looking at him whilst I did this.

"I don't think it's any of your business," I replied, knowing I was taking a big risk in not only collapsing a potential deal, but also getting myself a good kicking. He looked at me expressionless for a split second.

"Fair enough," he said. For the first time since I'd started talking to him, he hadn't looked unimpressed. My bold gamble had worked. Standing up to him had gained respect.

"What kind do you want?" He questioned. This wasn't getting any easier. My knowledge of ballistics was far from extensive. I took another sip of my beer to retain composure.

"Something small and easy to use," I replied.

"Thought you might say that," he said grinning and looking towards the girl. Unbelievably, I'd been so focused on the conversation that I'd temporarily forgotten she was there. She was smiling too. Innuendos about the size of my manhood in front of her were unfair, I thought. I used my brain and kept quiet though. He got something out of his pocket and handed it to me. It was a card with his name and title, "Entrepreneur", on it. His address and number were on it too. Entrepreneur, I repeated in my head and laughed inwardly

"Call me early next week and then we'll arrange a meet," he said.

"Early next week?" I questioned. I was hoping to get it quicker than this, I'd had my instructions for a week already. Jason detected my slight irritation.

"What's the matter?" he said a little aggressively.

"I was hoping to get it quicker than that," I replied, keeping up my bold act. For the first time since I'd come over, he looked angry, very angry, and it was not a pretty sight.

"This isn't a fucking sweet shop, man," he replied, not shouting but in a voice that had much anger to it. The guy next to me, Jason's mate, started laughing, but stopped when he saw Jason's expression was still deadly serious. I swallowed hard.

"Yeah, of course, sorry."

"You know how much they cost?" Jason asked, after a slight pause in which he seemed to calm himself down. I took another drink of beer. It was going down fast.

"Well, umm..."

"One K plus another hundred for ammo."

"Fine," I said, thinking it was a bit steep. However, I certainly wasn't brave or stupid enough to negotiate the price.

"I'll call you," I said. He nodded. I took one last look at the girl before I left. She smiled at me, a smile that actually made my heart flutter and the hairs on the back of my neck rise. I started to smile back at her but stopped myself, not wishing to look like I was flirting with her. I said, "Cheers," towards Jason and turned to walk away. I detected a quiet "bye" from the girl.

I downed the remainder of my pint as I walked slowly back around the bar and put the empty glass on a vacant table. I was gutted, as I thought I'd probably never get to see the girl again. I wondered if she was Jason's girlfriend or of one of the other blokes in their group. She was untouchable whatever, which increased my disappointment.

I spent most of my next week either worried about my next meet with Jason or what would happen to me if I didn't get myself to Wales soon to carry out my next hit. I wondered whether they'd have me under surveillance, following my movements. This was probably unlikely, although I suspected if nothing happened after a few weeks, they, whoever they were, would be in touch somehow.

When Monday arrived, my next dilemma was at what time to call Jason. I didn't want to hassle the guy for fear of upsetting him, but at the same time I needed to hurry this thing along. I decided I'd call him Monday evening. Once again, when I spoke to him, he seemed to have no recollection of me at all. After a couple of reminders, he finally remembered me. It worried me that he'd done nothing about getting my gun at all, but then he said it would be ready by Wednesday afternoon. His life intrigued me. How much of this type of dealing did he do? If he couldn't remember who I was each time I spoke to him, he was either dealing with many people or unreliable, which didn't bode well.

"I'll come around in the evening, shall I?

"No, two o'clock," he replied.

This, what with my job, was not convenient, but he'd said it in a way that stated it was not negotiable. I didn't like doing business with this guy. He was arrogant, rude and treated me like a nobody. However, I didn't really have a choice and therefore resisted my urge to voice my opinions to him. I had to expect as much in the business I was dealing in. I reluctantly agreed to his timing and the conversation ended abruptly. I'd rather not be asking my boss for more time off. I was already concerned about having to breach the subject of taking a few days off when I went to Wales. Still, I had no choice. My new work was my priority, and if I risked pissing my boss off to the point he might sack me, then so be it. If things went well, I didn't anticipate staying in the job for long anyway.

I made my way over to Jason's place after lunch on Wednesday afternoon, having memorised the way from my A to Z. He didn't live a long way away from me, but it wasn't an area I was familiar with. When I got there, I realised why it wasn't a place I went to very often. The picture of the area in my head wasn't a very good one, but seeing it was worse. It was a massive housing estate with numerous blocks of flats, which had been vandalised badly in places. Graffiti seemed to be everywhere there was a space for it. It had the appearance of a very depressing place to live in. I didn't emanate from the most salubrious of locations, but this was bordering upon concrete hell. I didn't understand it. Jason, with all his dealings, was probably a wealthy guy. Why didn't he live in a better area? I was perplexed by it, but I certainly wasn't going to ask him. I wasn't happy walking around the estate with eleven hundred pounds in my pocket either. It made me glad Jason had arranged the meet during the day. I would have felt even less secure during the dark of night.

It took me a while to locate his block and then flat. Signposts and door numbers were at a premium on Jason's estate. Fortunately, I was early so it didn't matter. In the absence of a doorbell or knocker, I rapped on the door with my knuckles. Thirty seconds later, I was repeating the act with more vigour. Surely, he wasn't out. A few seconds later, through the window of the door, I could make out a large silhouette of a man coming towards me. He peered at me for a few seconds before opening it, unnecessarily suspicious. I didn't recognise him at all from the pub I'd met Jason in the previous Wednesday night. Although that wasn't to say he wasn't there.

"I've come to see Jason," I said. He looked me up and down in a curious manner, maybe deciding whether I was worthy of my request. I was beginning to wonder if he could speak and was about to offer a further explanation of my appearance there when he stood to one side and signalled for me to enter with a tilt of the head.

Inside, the flat was nicely furnished with contemporary décor. This backed up my theory about Jason's wealth and also increased my curiosity as to why he lived in such a rundown area. The smell of cannabis hit me immediately. I was shown through a short passageway and into the lounge. There I saw Jason sitting on a very comfortable looking leather sofa. Rap music was playing from an expensive looking stack system. As I looked to the left of the room around the door, and to my surprise, I saw the girl from the pub. I did a double take and smiled at her.

"Hi," she smiled back at me, taking a drag from what appeared to be a joint.

Jason was on the phone and hadn't noticed my presence yet. I stood by the doorway, not quite sure what to do. The guy who'd answered the door had come in behind me and sat next to Jason on the sofa. This meant that the only remaining seat available was next to the girl on the sofa. I was just starting to move in that direction to take my place beside her when I heard another guy come in from behind me. I turned around and he stopped to look at me. His expression had a look that said *who the hell are you?* He didn't say anything though, in custom with the first guy, and instead walked past me and sat down next to the girl. He shuffled up close to her and put his hand on her knee. She took a long drag from the spliff and handed it over to him. Another well-built guy, he had a closely shaved head and an impressive tattoo of a Komodo dragon on his neck. None of the guys in this crowd were even average size, let alone small. I was feeling very uncomfortable standing in the middle of the room, completely incongruous. Jason was still talking on the phone and showing no signs of finishing his conversation; whether he'd registered my appearance in the room I had no idea, but I hadn't caught him look up at me yet. In the meantime, the three other occupants remained seated, occasionally looking at me and grinning to themselves. I felt a desperate urge to be out of there. The situation continued for what seemed like an eternity before one of them spoke. It was the guy who'd let me in. He started talking about what I assumed was a mutual friend who'd been stopped by the police in his car and had been done for "possession". He was discussing it with the guy who was on the other sofa with the girl. She was looking just as good as she did in the pub on the Wednesday beforehand. I felt better whilst this conversation was ongoing as the attention was not on me so much, even though I was still standing there looking like an idiot.

Finally, Jason's phone conversation ended, but even then, he didn't acknowledge me straight away. Instead, he briefly spoke to the others about his call. He didn't seem too pleased with the outcome of what he'd been discussing.

He got up and with a heavy sigh, walked past me, muttering "wait there, bro." I was hoping he was going to get the gun whilst he was gone; I didn't want to stay in this flat for any longer than absolutely necessary.

Whilst I stood there waiting for Jason to return, one of them addressed me. It took me by surprise, as I'd given up all hope of them talking to me. It was the girl. "I'm fascinated as to why you want it," she said.

"Why?" I replied.

"You just don't seem the type," she responded.

"Why doesn't he?" piped up her boyfriend, seeming a little perturbed that she was talking to me. "Just because he doesn't look like the type, doesn't mean to say he doesn't have issues with people. Remember, the quiet ones are the worst."

"I don't agree," she argued. "Some people just don't get involved in this sort of business and he looks like one of them."

"What do you know anyway? The proof to my point is that he's here. That means people who look like him do get involved." He looked pleased with himself over this comment.

I stood there quietly whilst this conversation was ongoing. I felt like a child whose parents were talking about it. They bickered for a bit longer before she asked me again why I wanted a gun, maybe wanting to try to settle the disagreement with the truth. I was thinking about my response when fortunately, Jason came back in the room, saving me having to reply. As he did, everyone went quiet. He was clearly the alpha male in the group and ruled the roost. There was no real reason for it, as the other two guys were just as big as Jason. However, he seemed to have an aura that made you fearful of him. As he sat back down, the room was silent, waiting for him to speak, like a tribe waiting for their leader to address them. Jason placed a revolver on the table along with a box.

"Take a look," he said. I went over to the table, leaned down and picked up the gun. It was reasonably heavy considering its size. I inwardly joked about asking whether it came with a manual. I didn't know what to look for. For all I knew it could have been a good fake. I looked at it closely and held it out as if to fire it. I was hoping these actions would give them the impression I knew a small bit about guns. I looked at Jason and said, "Good."

Jason rubbed his thumb against his fingers to indicate money. I pulled the wedge of cash out that I'd taken there in my pocket. Even though I was pretty sure I was paying well over the odds for the gun, I was happy to be rid of some cash. I had so much lying around at home at the moment. I laid the money on the table. Jason remained sitting back on the sofa. He obviously trusted me enough not to count it. More likely he didn't believe I'd be stupid enough to try to do him over. I picked up the box which I assumed held the bullets. I suddenly realised I had nothing to put the gun and box in to carry them out of here.

"Have you got a bag?" I asked and instantly regretted the question. It was met with laughs and sniggers all around the room. The girl was looking at her boyfriend as if to say, *I told you he wasn't cut out for this.*

"Fucking hell," sighed Jason in disbelief. "This guy's unreal." He paused for a second and then said, "Somebody get this dick a bag," looking at me as though sympathetic to my stupidity. The girl jumped up, still grinning, and went out of the room.

I said, "Cheers," as I turned to follow her. Nobody replied. I waited in the hall for her. I was feeling relieved that I was about to be out of there. She came back holding a carrier bag that didn't look like it would disguise my gun very well. She walked past me to the door and opened it. She's more polite than the others, I thought, admiring her once more, especially now I was out of sight of Jason and his crew. She gave me the bag and I placed the gun and the box in it whilst she stood there. I was about to leave when she handed me a small slip of paper. Written on it was

"Kez," and a phone number.

"I need to know why you've bought that," she said and smiled, looking at the bag. I looked back at her, not knowing what to say. I walked out the door, remaining dumbstruck.

"Take care, it's dangerous out there," she said sarcastically as I trudged off. The act of giving me her number had completely thrown me and took my mind off the fact that I was walking around in broad daylight with a gun and ammunition. I couldn't believe she'd given me her number. Surely her motives couldn't be just to find out what I was up to. She'd also done it privately away from her bloke, although I felt certain she couldn't be interested in me. Perhaps she was just amused by me and thought it would be fun to find out more. I'd already made up my mind that I'd call her though. I knew it was probably a dangerous thing to do, given that her boyfriend was huge and had psycho friends, but my life seemed to be getting more and more dangerous by the minute. Although, I had a lot to be worried about I was beginning to enjoy the buzz of living on the edge.

On Thursday morning, I phoned my boss to tell him I was too ill to come to work and said I wasn't sure when I'd be back. I packed a few things and headed down to South Wales. I was hoping that I'd have the job complete by the end of the weekend. I'd decided not to call Kez beforehand. I didn't want to look too keen and I didn't know her intentions, so I made up my mind I'd resist the urge and call her upon my return from South Wales.

Driving down to Neath, I was aware that I needed to try the gun out at least once. I wanted to test it to make sure I could work it before I put myself in a situation to use it for real. I diverted my journey to a country lane that seemed well off the beaten track. I parked the car and was as confident as I could be that there wasn't anybody around to see what I was doing. Anybody that may hear me in the distance might think the gunshot was that of a farmer. I found a tree that looked good for practice and took aim. Two shots later and I was happy I knew how to handle the weapon. Even the recoil wasn't as bad as I expected it to be. Perhaps I was a natural. I got out of there quickly and back on the road to Wales.

I checked myself into a dive of a hotel that night and started looking up where I'd find Paul Donaldson, my next target. I went to see his house for myself that evening. Paul lived on the outskirts of the town centre in a decent sized semi-detached house. There was an Audi parked in the drive. He seemed a step up from Julie McParland. From the look of his house and judging by his age, he looked like he could be a family man.

I returned to the road early the next day and waited like I had done for Julie. I felt more uneasy as the morning drifted by and there was no movement from his house, his car remaining in the drive. I didn't like the fact quite a few people may have walked past and noted me waiting in the car, even if I had taken the precaution of parking a few doors down from Paul's house.

I waited there for a few hours, but nothing happened. I decided to cut my loses and returned to my hotel. I'd try again later. I decided to put my afternoon to use. Sitting, waiting in my car had got me thinking. This would be the sort of thing police would be after and ask about if they were investigating a murder - strangers hanging around. I was now paranoid; if I didn't make myself less conspicuous, I'd be caught. I decided to get a new identity. I bought a hat and some new clothes that I wouldn't normally dream of wearing. I also got a pair of glasses that just had clear non-magnifying glass in. I returned in my new attire later that evening. This time I parked a good mile away and walked to the house from there. My target lived on a small housing estate. The problem I had was that I couldn't loiter around. I needed to get lucky and catch him coming out of his house and follow him somewhere, perhaps a place of work where I could monitor him more easily. Once again, I had no luck in seeing him that evening, not that I hung about for long.

Over the next few days, I kept trying but to no avail. I didn't see the guy once. I did develop a reasonably good plan to watch him though. There was a bus stop a street away from where he lived. Looking at the geography of his area, going past this bus stop would be the mostly likely route he'd take from his house by either car or on foot, irrespective of where he was going. I'd wait at the bus stop a couple of times a day for a while before eventually getting on a bus. I thought waiting at a bus stop would render me more oblivious to the locals.

Eventually, after a few days I got my break. It was around eight o'clock in the evening when I saw my man walk past. I followed him at a comfortable distance behind. I was pleased that I'd seen him when it was dark. He walked for about fifteen minutes until I saw him enter a building which was a drinking club. I didn't follow him inside; I decided to go and get something to eat instead. I'd return a little later. The chances were he'd be in there for at least a couple of hours. I sat in a fast-food place, planning my move. I wanted to get this over and done with, given that I didn't know when I'd get my next opportunity. This guy didn't seem to have a regular job or an established pattern of leaving or returning to his house. Either this or I'd just missed him and had been unlucky. This seemed as good as chance as any. Firstly, I figured he'd be drinking and therefore a little more off guard. My theory being that it was a reasonable walk from his house to the club and he would have driven if he wasn't intending on having at least a couple of pints. Secondly, there was a small alleyway I'd followed him through on the way and it was likely he'd return that way as well. This would be a very good place to carry out my assassination. It wasn't perfect because the surrounding area was quite well built up. However, I'd noticed that the houses that backed onto the alleyway were shielded by a large wall either side, probably put there to keep the privacy of their gardens.

I dragged out my meal before leaving and going on a slow walk to kill time. Eventually, I made my way back to the drinking club and waited across the road, sheltered in a shop doorway. Just before eleven o'clock, I saw him come out with another man who appeared to be in the same age group. They chatted for a minute or so before they parted their ways, Paul heading in the direction back to his house and the other guy going the opposite way. I was now on the prowl. Adrenaline was pumping around my body and I felt nervous. It felt different from the first time. Despite my fears and worries, there was also an element of anticipation and even excitement. I wanted to do it.

As I followed him back along the route we'd taken on the way there, I was concerned that there would be somebody around when we got to the alleyway. If there was anyone within sight I'd have to abort.

I kept a distance from him at first, but as we got nearer to my chosen action point, I started to close the gap. The weather was on my side. In the last twenty minutes a thin drizzle had started to fall. This would hopefully prevent more people from walking about as well as reduce vision. As we approached the alleyway, I pulled the gun from where I'd tucked it into my waist and held onto it firmly inside my coat so it was not visible. I started to think about all the things that could go wrong. I might have trouble firing the gun or miss my target; after all, I'd only practised with it once before. Maybe then he'd disarm me. Or perhaps he might escape. I knew I needed to get the job done tonight. If he escaped, I might not get another chance, as he would be on his guard and the police would likely be looking for me. Lastly, even if I did carry out the shooting successfully, I might not get away. A loud gunshot could be heard by many people in a built-up area such as this one and I might be seen escaping. I had to put all of this to the back of my mind though.

My heart was pumping fast, and my legs felt like jelly as the alleyway came into view. I had more time to think about it than the first hit. That had been a spur of the moment thing, which meant I wasn't considering the possible consequences of my actions.

As we entered the alleyway, I was only a few metres behind him. I guessed the alleyway was about seventy-five metres long. I didn't have much time to act. I looked all around. I was in luck. I could see no one else either end of the alleyway. I quickened my pace once more and took the gun out from my coat. My palms were sweaty and I struggled to get a good firm grip on the gun, which was also compounded by my slight shaking as well.

I ideally wanted to shoot him when we were in the middle of the alley, as it felt more secure there somehow. Thinking about it afterwards, I realised that this was wrong and that it would have been better to do it at one end so that I could get away out of the alley quicker. I was very close to him by the time he turned around. He must have been able to feel my presence directly behind him. He looked at me suspiciously at first, but this changed to fear and horror when I raised the gun. I fired my first shot just as it appeared he was going to speak. I followed this with two more quick shots. Gruesomely, there was blood and flesh spraying around. I was at point blank range and couldn't miss; he fell to the ground like a lifeless object. I didn't stop to check him once he fell. I was happy that the job was done.

The shots had been loud, almost deafening. To anyone within earshot, it must have been obvious what it was. There was no way you could have mistaken it for anything else, like a firework or a car backfiring. I knew that people in the surrounding houses would be looking out of their windows or even coming out of them to see what was going on. I tucked the gun back into my waist and ran away from where his body lay. This was another area I'd been amateurish in as I hadn't planned a definitive escape route. I just kept running, not even certain of where I was going, after a minute or two of running I saw someone on the other side of the road to that I was on. I kept my head down and slowed to a walk. I was still in the housing estate and heading in the opposite direction to where my hotel was situated.

I eventually found my way to a main road where I was able to double back on myself. My hotel was a couple of miles away, but I didn't want to get the bus back because I didn't want to be seen in the area by anyone. People would get a better view of me on a lit bus. Instead, I walked back to the hotel which took me the best part of an hour.

I slept badly that night. I tried to erase the sight of what the bullets had done to his face, but I struggled. Overall, it wasn't as bad as last time. I wasn't as worried or as paranoid. That isn't to say I enjoyed the next few days though.

I checked out of my hotel two days after the hit and made my way back to London. When I arrived back home, I found my boss had left me a message on my answer machine at home. He didn't sound too pleased with my lack of appearances at work recently. I realised it was time to give up my day job. I would become a full-time assassin.

Although, like the first time, I avoided all media so as not to hear anything about the murder I'd committed, there was no escaping it. I'd catch a glimpse of his picture in someone's newspaper when I was out, or his face would appear on television in the pub. It seemed as though this murder was more high profile. I was tempted to try and find out why but thought it better for my sanity to keep as far removed from it as possible.

I'd been away in Wales for over a week. I got questioned from friends and family as to where I'd been. Even though the lying came easy, it was not something I enjoyed. When I told my boss I was giving up work, he was none too pleased, calling me a good-for-nothing amongst a tirade of expletives. This made me all the more pleased I was packing it in. Although I realised I hadn't been the model employee recently, I'd wanted to give it up for ages and felt the workers were generally treated poorly. It was therefore a goal achieved. Despite the happiness of being freed from the job, I did have a nagging doubt at the back of my mind. It was a security thing in that, even though I had a lot of cash, I didn't know how long it would last. I certainly couldn't go back to that job; I'd burned my bridges there.

Chapter Six

About a week after I'd completed my mission, payment came through. The process was like clockwork. It was all so simple. By this time, my paranoia had subsided once again, and I felt more free and easy walking about. It started to look like I'd got away with it again.

During this time, Kez had been on my mind and the idea of phoning her. Whilst I was worried about being caught or linked to the murder of Paul, I decided not to contact her, but since I started to feel better about the situation, I decided it was time. My thoughts since I'd last seen her had not changed, I wanted to phone her and meet up if possible. I remembered how attractive I found her. I sat in my flat, the phone at my side, looking at her number. I didn't know what I would say to her. Although she'd given me her number, I struggled to believe that she'd done it because she genuinely wanted to see me again. It could be a wind up; after all, she had a boyfriend and on the two occasions I'd seen her, I'd been made to look stupid by her friends. I dialled her number, it kept ringing and then clicked on to answer phone. An automated message, similar to that of my new employers, told me to leave a message. I obeyed its request and left my number for her to call me back. I preferred it this way. The ball was now in her court and I knew that if she was genuinely interested, she'd phone me. If not then fine, at least I'd know where I stood.

That night I went to the Crooked Billet. I'd been there a couple of times since my return from Wales, but I'd not had a big night there, as on those occasions I'd been fielding questions about my recent whereabouts, and this had driven me away early. However, that night was one of those nights, even though it was only a Wednesday, where everyone you knew seemed to turn up. I was in a buoyant mood, even before I'd touched a drop of alcohol. Receiving the money for my work and also having inwardly self-declared myself free from the danger of being caught from the crime had put me on a high. I was drunk very quickly though. I'd been a little out of practice recently and this, coupled with my good feeling, meant the alcohol went to my head quickly. I soon started buying all my mates drinks. A couple of my ex-work mates were there also, and they were perplexed as to how I'd packed in my job, seemingly remained out of work, but was flashing money around.

I persuaded a few of my mates to go onto a nightclub once the pub had closed. From there, my memory of the night became hazy. The only thing that was clear was that I was very drunk by the time I left.

The next morning, sleeping off my exploits, I was awoken by the phone. Fortunately, I'd just had a phone point installed in my bedroom, otherwise I don't think I would have heard it. As I answered it, I was already regretting my actions the night before, I felt terrible.

"Hi," a female voice said.

"Hi," I responded, not knowing who it was.

"It's Kez," the girl said. "You phoned me last night. I'd given up on you phoning me to be honest."

"I've been busy, sorry," I said, feeling like I'd been told off. There was then a pause. This wasn't really the time for me to be talking to her. My brain felt pickled and I lacked the concentration to have even a basic phone conversation.

"So, have you been playing cowboys and Indians then?" She asked. I laughed. Had she phoned to mock me? The cogs in my mind were working on how I could get her off the phone. I wanted to speak to her later when I was much more compos mentis.

"Do you fancy going out for dinner on Sunday?" she said, before I could say anything.

"Yeah, sure," I responded in surprise. I hadn't been expecting her to ask me out like that.

"I'll book a table at The Plaza for eight o'clock. You know it?"

This girl doesn't hang about, I thought. She's to the point.

"Yes," I replied. I'd never been there but I'd heard of it. It was quite expensive from what I knew.

"See you there then," she said and with that she hung up, leaving me to dwell on our brief conversation. It had all seemed rather surreal. However, I was looking forward to Sunday already. Knowing that she wanted to see me was fantastic. Although, I knew it was another danger I was adding to my life that I was already living on the edge. Her boyfriend and his mates didn't seem very nice people, especially if wronged. I'm sure they wouldn't take too kindly to me having a meal with Kez, and I didn't like to think what they might do to me should they find out. This all added to the buzz of it. Not only was she stunning, I was risking my health at the same time. The existence I'd created for myself in recent times made me feel alive. I'd tried living a normal life and it didn't work. Despite the stress, the lies and the risk of it all going wrong, I didn't regret my actions. I already felt I had more of a legacy from my life during the last couple of months than I had beforehand.

As I lay in bed craving water and headache tablets, but not

having the energy to go and get them, I did have some concerns regarding the previous night. I was very drunk and it worried me that I may have mentioned something I shouldn't have to one of my mates. This was something I'd have to be conscious of in the future.

Sunday evening came around, and admittedly I was nervous about it. Even though Kez had made all the running so far, I didn't trust the situation and was wondering whether she was somehow leading me into some sort of trap. I thought she was too good-looking to be interested in me.

I turned up at the restaurant on time and she was already seated at a table waiting for me. It felt like a clandestine meeting from a scene out of a film as I walked over to where she was. I said "hello," and sat down. Kez looked as good as I'd remembered. She'd made a bit of an effort with more make-up on than I'd seen her with before. She wore a green tank top over a white blouse. She'd put her hair in a ponytail. She at once took the lead and asked me what I'd done over the weekend. I decided she wasn't the sort of girl you could dominate or dictate to. In fact, she was probably a control freak.

My weekend hadn't been at all interesting. I'd had a couple of beers with my mates, perused the shops out of boredom on Saturday and otherwise lazed around my flat watching television. I rebounded this question, which seemed an obvious thing to do, but she didn't answer me. Instead, she grinned and said, "I've already ordered a drink for you. I hope you don't mind?"

"No, well, I suppose it depends what it is."

"Gin and tonic. I'm really into them at the moment. It doesn't seem right having dinner without having one. Did you drive here?" she asked.

I'd been indecisive about whether to drive or not. The

restaurant she'd suggested was a pain for me to get to by public transport and even though I could now afford taxis, it always seemed a waste of money. After deliberating, I'd reluctantly decided to drive. "Yes, but I could always leave the car here if I have one too many."

She held my gaze for a while but didn't say anything. I thought that perhaps she was calculating in her mind what sort of a person I was. At that point, the waiter came and asked if we were ready to order. I was just about to ask for a couple more minutes to decide when Kez said she was ready and reeled off her order. I read the menu quickly and made my order without giving it much thought. Once the waiter had gone there was silence between us. I looked around the restaurant, something I hadn't really had the opportunity to do before. It was busy, but not full. It had a nice atmosphere to it, was softly lit and well decorated. Tables were mainly dominated by couples like Kez and I, although they looked like proper couples. I had no idea what we could be described as or what the future held for us. It was a good place to impress a prospective partner, although I wasn't sure this was Kez's reason for choosing it. I looked back at Kez who had seemingly been eyeing me whilst I scanned our surroundings.

"How long have you been going out with your boyfriend?" I asked her. I didn't want there being any pretense that she didn't have a boyfriend, which I could see developing. Better to face the facts. The question seemed to temporarily perturb her, evident through the brief frown that appeared on her face. However, she quickly recovered the grin which she'd pretty much had on her face since I'd arrived. It was a grin that showed amusement, bordering on being condescending.

"What made you think I've got a boyfriend?" she asked.

This question annoyed me. It had been obvious back at Jason's flat that the guy she'd been sitting next to was her boyfriend and this just confirmed my fears that she was playing games with me. However, at the same time, her looks pacified my anger. They had a hold on me that meant I couldn't treat her just like anyone else. I thought of my ex-girlfriend and mentally compared the two. My ex hadn't been as naturally good looking as Kez, but there was something about her I found very attractive. It was her little movements, like the way she held herself whilst standing or how she walked. She didn't try to be sexy, which suited her. In fact, what I really liked about her was that I was attracted to her, but I thought that most other men probably wouldn't give her much of a second glance. They would see her as ordinary, not the way that I saw her. I suppose that was what made her unique and special. On top of that she was a nice, fun person. Whereas Kez was just stunning. She had looks that would turn any bloke's head in the street. I couldn't imagine myself ever going out with a girl as beautiful as her. Although she could probably be a real bitch, she was also interesting. I imagined a relationship with her wouldn't be boring. She'd be a real challenge to keep hold of. Kez seemed like the sort of girl you had a bit of fun with and moved on, whereas my ex-girlfriend was marriage material.

"Well, you seemed pretty friendly with that guy at Jason's flat," I replied. She didn't respond to this, but her eyes remained on me. I had the urge to say something else to break the uncomfortable silence.

"What would he do if he knew we were here together?" I asked her.

"Oh, he'd probably have you put in a wheelchair," she replied in a very matter-of-fact way. This was more than believable from what I'd seen of him and his mates, but part of me also felt that she'd said this to see the effect it had on me.

"And what would he do to you?"

"Don't know. He wouldn't be happy, but it would be you who I'd be worried about," she said.

"Worried about?" I questioned. Once again, she didn't reply. We sat in silence for a few seconds.

"Why did you want to see me?" I asked.

"You're very inquisitive," she said in a disapproving tone. "I've already told you that."

"To find out why I bought that…" I stopped, realising we were in a public place. She giggled at this.

"Yes," she said. "You seem so innocent. You don't look like the sort of guy who'd need a weapon. I see you more of the 'still living at home with Mum' type."

I ignored this patronising comment.

"What makes you think I'm going to tell you?"

"Oh, you will."

This time it was my turn to sit there and grin back at her, whilst not saying anything. A few seconds later, the waiter brought our starters. Once we tucked into our food, the mood seemed to relax a bit; we talked about our pasts. Although, she failed to mention how she got caught up with Jason and co. As I'd suspected, she was a good laugh and easy to talk to. She'd done courses on fitness instruction but was currently in between jobs. She must therefore be a kept woman. She did seem genuinely interested in me. I hadn't told her how I was "officially unemployed," lying to her that I was still in my building job. I was even lying now when I didn't need to.

Once we'd finished our meal, we ordered a bottle of wine so that we could stay there chatting. Starting to feel the effects of the alcohol, I asked her about how she got to know Jason. I thought she wasn't going to divulge anything at first, but then she started to open up.

"I met Gaz, my boyfriend, first. I didn't know Jason and the rest before then. Gaz and I met in a nightclub about a year ago. He's a good laugh and I soon discovered he wasn't short of a few quid. He treated me well, dining me regularly and seeing that I never had to pay for anything. At first, I was naive and didn't realise where he got his money from, but then as I gradually got introduced to his mates, I worked out that he wasn't a nine to five office worker. I didn't want to ask what he got up to and I still don't know the full picture. As I've got to know him more, I've picked up snippets of information that he has told me as well as overhearing him talking to his mates. He's involved in large supply drug dealing. I think Jason's one of the top dogs in the operation. It makes Gaz quite a tidy sum, though. They also, as you know through your business, have side-lines as well.

"Jason's a nightclub bouncer, isn't he? Surely he doesn't need to do that if he's making a fortune out of drugs."

"Yeah, but I think that's how he started up. A lot of his contacts are known through the job, as well as being close to supply lines. You're probably right; he doesn't need the money from it. It's a hobby or a habit I reckon. Gaz does a bit as well."

"Bouncer work?"

"Yeah, that's how we met."

"So, you approve of what they do then?" I asked.

"I don't give a shit really, it's their business."

"But you're taking the money from him."

"So what? Anyway, you're not Mr Innocent yourself. Buying guns isn't legal, is it?"

This was a fair point that firmly stopped my argument.

Sometimes I completely forgot what I'd done and who I was. I saw myself as innocent, which must have been a subconscious way of erasing any guilt I was feeling about killing people.

"Talking of which, you haven't told me your business with that yet."

"I didn't say I was going to," I replied.

"Come on. I've just told you a lot about me," Kez pressed.

"Not now. Maybe another time." Kez looked pissed off with this response.

"Are you worried I'm going to grass you up or something?"

"No, it's not that. It's complicated and I'm not ready to talk about it."

She reluctantly accepted this.

When it came to paying the bill, I was surprised, as I thought she would expect me to pay. Instead, we agreed to go halves rather than arguing. The irony of two supposedly unemployed people arguing to pay a rather large bill for a meal wasn't lost on me. Both of our funds had been through ill-gotten ways. As we got up to leave, I asked Kez a question.

"So, are you intending to stick with Gaz for a while then?"

"Why's it of interest to you?" Kez replied. I'd walked into that response, which I think had also been fuelled by the fact I'd refused to talk to her about the gun. Outside the restaurant, Kez said she was going to get a cab home. Even though I hadn't expected an invite back to her place, I had to hide my disappointment. I'd had far too much to drink to drive back home and although it was tempting, I knew I should get a cab as well. It wasn't like I didn't have the time to come back and get my car the next day.

Realising we weren't easily going to get two cabs standing

outside, we went back into the restaurant and asked them to phone for taxis for us. It wasn't worth us sharing one as we lived in opposite directions. We sat at a vacant table whilst we waited. The restaurant was almost empty, and the night had the feel that it was over. I was half tempted to ask Kez if she wanted to go somewhere else. This wasn't just because I wanted to spend more time with her, but also because I wasn't in the mood for going home. However, since the gun conversation she'd not been so friendly, and I knew it was almost certain she'd say no.

"What made you choose this restaurant then?" I asked.

"I've been here a couple of times and I liked it," she replied. "Where do you normally take you girlfriends?" she asked.

"I don't know. Nowhere classy. Pub, cinema, maybe for a pizza if I want to impress them."

"You know how to treat a girl," she joked.

We sat there for a few more minutes before a waiter came to tell us our taxis were outside. I looked at Kez, not knowing what to say, was this the end or would we meet again? She was certainly in control of the situation. I felt her put her hand on my arm and pull me gently towards her. We kissed briefly, but long enough for it not to be mistaken for a friendly goodbye kiss. We broke apart and she smiled at me. My heart was pumping fast and I was trying to take in what had happened. I wanted to continue the kiss but knew I couldn't because the cabs were waiting. She looked like she was ready to go.

"Enjoy playing cowboys and Indians," she joked. "I've got more to find out more about you, which I suspect is what you want. I'll call you, and next time you can thrill me with a night out in one of your pubs." She said goodbye and kissed me, this time with just a peck on the lips. She turned away and walked to her cab. I watched her as she got into the back of it. She never once turned back to look at me. I got into the front of my taxi and proceeded to make small talk with the driver all the way home.

I awoke the next morning, my body covered with sweat after a bad dream. It was strange, because going to bed I'd been on a real high. The evening I'd spent with Kez had been unusual, but I'd enjoyed it. I was still pleasantly surprised we'd kissed and that she'd said she would call me to meet up again. However, my restless night brought home to me the risks I was taking. I'd murdered two people in the last couple of months and could possibly get caught at any time. I'd undoubtedly be asked to kill again, and who knows what would happen to me if I refused. On top of this, I'd just started seeing the girlfriend of a major drug dealer who'd probably seriously disable me if he found out. Despite this, I liked this life. Nobody I knew would have one like it.

Over the next few days, my life levelled out to a more normal existence. Nothing out of the ordinary happened. I checked the post office for any assignments and there were none. There was no call from Kez. After everything that had happened to me, it was a bit of a come down, even though I probably needed it. Although I liked the idea of being able to relax and not have anything imminent to worry about, in truth I was bored. I also found that having time on my hands made me more edgy. If I was out, I was looking around to see if anyone was following me. On the odd occasion there was a knock at my door, I'd be virtually in a cold sweat by the time I'd opened it.

The boredom did allow me time to think, though. I realised that I couldn't sit around doing nothing, waiting for another envelope to appear in my mail at the post office. I had to find something to occupy my time. The idea of being a man of leisure didn't have the appeal I'd first attached to it. I thought about what

I could do. I certainly didn't want to go back into the building trade, which was the only thing I had experience in. After giving it some thought, I came up with the perfect job. I'd take up lorry driving. I knew a guy, a while back, who'd left his job to do the same thing. It would suit me well, because a lot of the jobs were agency work which meant I could pick and choose what I did to a certain extent. It would also explain away my disappearances. Whenever I went away for a few days, I could tell anyone who asked that I was away on a lorry driving job. My life would make a lot more sense to people looking at it from the outside if I started driving for a living. I was already getting several questions from friends and family regarding what I was going to do and how I was coping financially, being unemployed.

Another advantage would be security. If the assassination work dried up, I would have something to fall back on. I'd always fancied being a lorry driver; it seemed reasonably well paid and—I hoped—secure. I'd have to pass my HGV licence, which cost money, but that was something I wasn't short of.

I used my spare time to look into the process and booked a course, the first of a couple I needed to take to be able to drive the largest of lorries.

Another thing on my mind during those days was my last murder scene. Things went to plan, but I couldn't get the noise of the gunshots out of my mind. It must certainly have alerted many people around, thereby significantly increasing my chances of being caught. Up until now, it looked as though I may have got away with it, but if I kept on carrying out hits like this it would only be a matter of time before I was caught. I decided the way round it was to get a gun with a silencer. It would allow me to carry out my work without attracting as much attention as I may have got last time. My problem was where to get one. I could go back to Jason; he was the obvious place to start. I had doubts about this though. Firstly, I wasn't certain he could get one. Kez had said that guns were just a side-line and he didn't give the impression, when I was dealing with him, he had numerous models to offer. Also, now having met Kez, I'd rather avoid Jason, Gaz and co. if possible. However, despite this, I had no idea who else to go to. The only other thing was maybe speaking to Kez about it. Although, if I was to do this, I'd have no option other than to tell her my whole business with guns. This would mean placing a lot of trust in her. She'd also then have to obtain the gun whilst hiding the identity of who it was for. Also, Kez, by her own admission, didn't know too much about Jason's business and didn't get involved, so the request would seem strange coming from her. It would be unlikely she'd know up front whether this was the sort of thing they could get anyway. I had to think of something, though, as I wanted this type of gun and felt it was necessary to the continued success of my new trade.

It had been a while since I'd seen Kez and my confidence on whether she was going to call me was waning. She'd been on my mind a lot since I'd last seen her, so if she didn't call, I'd be gutted. I wanted to see her again so I could get to know her more. We'd had a good night out and she was funny and interesting despite being aloof at times. I was undoubtedly attracted to the dangers of having a relationship with her as well.

I continued to spend time racking my brains about how I could get my hands on a silencer without going through Jason. I thought about all my mates and people I knew from the Crooked Billet. Some of them were a bit dodgy, in that they weren't averse to selling stolen goods and dabbling in drugs, but I didn't think any of them were involved in anything as heavy as guns. I'm sure if I asked around enough, sooner or later I'd find somebody who knew someone who could help me. The problem was I didn't want to put the word out about it. I needed to keep my new life a secret and asking around randomly for guns would certainly jeopardise this. I'd been lucky the first time around that Brad had managed to put me in touch with Jason. He'd been suspicious of me at first, but he believed my lies about it being for someone else and now had seemingly forgotten about the whole episode.

I was beginning to think I'd have to go through Jason and if I did how would I approach it, when out of the blue Kez called me. She talked to me as normal, not mentioning our last night out, or that it had been over a week ago. She took control once again and told me to name a pub we could meet in on Thursday night. I suggested one I used to go to with my ex-girlfriend. It was quiet and good for couples. There was no way I was meeting her at the Crooked Billet under the scrutiny of all my mates and people I knew in there. Kez didn't chat for long. Once the time and place of our meet was agreed, she ended the call. This didn't stop me feeling like a love-struck teenager after I'd put the phone down. Each time I thought she wasn't interested, she proved me wrong. I wondered whether she was restricted as to when she could see or speak to me because of Gaz. It was a strong possibility.

Now that Kez had called, it had put a new dimension to my gun silencer dilemma. Did I try to go through Kez? Or at least see if she could get me any information on the subject? Also, if I decided not to go through her but to Jason direct, would I tell her, as chances were she'd find out anyway? I still hadn't decided upon the question when I entered The Greyhound, the pub we were meeting in. Once again, Kez was there already. She was either hot on punctuality or keen. She was sat in one corner of the pub, a bottle of beer sitting in front of her. She took a swig from the bottle as I walked up to her. Her greeting wasn't overly warm; she stayed in her seat and smiled at me in a way that suggested she was pleased to see me as a source of amusement to her, rather than genuinely wanting to see me. I got myself a drink from the bar and sat down opposite her. The pub was quiet, as I'd thought it would be. She looked around and said "nice," in a sarcastic way.

"Well, it's better than that dive your mob hang out in on Wednesdays," I snapped back. She said nothing, not rising to the bait.

At first, our conversation was like starting all over again. We'd not seemed to regain any of the rapport we'd built the last time we were out. She asked me what I'd been up to since we'd last met. I told her it hadn't been a lot and that it was generally uninteresting. She kept quiet once I'd finished saying this, so I found myself telling her about my plans to become a lorry driver. I regretted this immediately, as I realised as I was telling her how boring it would sound and very unimpressive. Not that this meant I wanted to do it any less, that was part of the appeal. I was still of the opinion that it was perfect for my situation, preventing boredom and explaining away my sudden disappearances. Despite her looking bored as I told her my plans, she questioned me about it.

"I've got a lot to learn about you. Why does that interest you?" she asked. I'd dug myself into a rut, because I wasn't ready to give her the main reason.

"Because it's something I've always wanted to do. It pays well, I'll have time to think and I get to go places." I responded defensively. She laughed at my last point.

"Are you ambitious?"

"Yeah, of course."

"Well, why are you doing a lorry driver's course then?" She'd responded as I suspected her to: belittling.

"Just because I'm doing this now, doesn't mean to say I haven't got ambitions or plans to do other things in the future," I said, on the defensive again.

"What are your long-term ambitions then? Kez asked.

"Christ, I feel like I'm in a job interview."

"I'm just interested," she replied. "This sort of thing tells you a lot about a person"

"I don't know what I'm going to do long-term. I'm still young; I've got plenty of time to sort it out." Kez smiled at me, but it had a condescending air to it that I ignored. She didn't really know me.

"Do you plan to be a kept woman then? I replied, partly because I wanted to have a little dig at her.

"Don't know. Although it's got its advantages, I just spent the last week wasted and didn't have to pay for a penny of it."

"But in my defence, because I feel like you're having a dig at me, you don't have a clue what you're going to do in the future."

She laughed, "You shouldn't take things so personally. I only questioned you because I'm interested and if it seems as though I'm criticising you, it's because I think you can do better."

I was taken back by this comment, as it was a bit more heartfelt and genuine than I'd come to expect from her.

We made small talk for a while before she went to the toilet. On the way back she bought some drinks. Whilst she'd been gone, I'd been sitting there thinking about our relationship. This was only the second time we'd met, but it was obvious she was interested in me to some extent, despite her sometimes cold and patronising ways towards me. She'd made all the running as well as kissed me at the end of our last night out. I decided to question her more about Gaz and her plans.

"Do you think you'll stay with Gaz then?"

"Well, it helps buy the drinks," she laughed, eyeing my pint.

"Yeah, but in all seriousness, you can't be madly in love with him if you're sitting here with me, can you?"

"Don't flatter yourself," she said to me, seemingly exasperated at my comment. "Anyway, who said I was in love with him. There are many things I like about Gaz. He's different; he doesn't have a run-of-the-mill life. I think he might be going places, and so what if his dealings are illegal? On top of all that, he gives me shit loads of cash. I'll probably stick with him until I get a better offer," she said, looking at me. I wanted to tell her how shallow I thought this all sounded, but I didn't want to get her back up.

"Sounds romantic," I joked instead.

"I don't really believe in romance. I don't think it happens in the real world," she replied. I didn't disagree with her.

I looked around our surroundings and said, "This is the epitome of romance."

"My case proven," she said. "So, have you got a girlfriend?"

"No."

"When did you last have one?"

"A few months back."

"Why did you split up?"

"Not sure really, she said it was time to move on," I replied. I didn't want to be talking about it, but Kez had had annoyingly sensed straight away it was something I wasn't happy about and wanted to know more.

"Did you think that?"

"No, at the time I was happy, but looking back, maybe she was right."

Kez looked at me inquisitively but didn't say anything.

"I don't think it would have lasted in the long run," I added.

"It hurt you, didn't it?" she said with a hint of sympathy, although I wasn't sure if she was being sincere. I didn't respond to this. Instead, I changed the subject by offering Kez another drink, even though she hadn't finished her last one. This would give her the message the subject was closed.

We carried on talking about our past and our views on certain things. In many ways we had a lot in common. Our talk was very natural, especially the more we had to drink. Kez opened up to me as well. She'd had a difficult childhood, which I can't say surprised me. Her dad had died when she was eight years old, not leaving much money and therefore her family had been poor. Her mum hadn't been too nice either by all accounts. It was probably the stress and strain of trying to get through life, but she took it out on Kez. I reckoned this was why Kez had turned out to be tough and cold, what some of my mates and I would describe as a hard bitch. She'd shown a softer side of herself to me, though.

Throughout the night, I toyed with the idea of telling Kez about my real life. I wanted to do it, not just so I could ask her if she could get me a silencer, but also because I wanted to talk to someone about it and in many ways, she seemed the ideal person. However, each time I thought about it, I realised how serious a thing it was and couldn't convince myself what she'd think, or how she'd react and even whether I could trust her.

Before we knew it, last orders were being called at the bar and shortly afterwards we found ourselves outside the pub without a plan of what to do next. I didn't want to go home, but I was expecting we'd part our separate ways and was waiting for

Kez to take the lead once more.

"You hungry?" she said.

"I could do with something to eat." Although I'd eaten earlier, the beers had created a superficial hunger in me.

"Do you want to come back to mine? I fancy cooking some pasta."

"OK," I said rather too eagerly to this spur of the moment proposal that caught me totally by surprise. We headed in the direction of the bus stop.

"I thought you lived with Gaz," I said.

"I do," she replied and looked at me to see the alarm on my face. "He loves pasta." She waited a few seconds to see my reaction. I didn't know what to say.

"We're not going back to where I live, though. I'm house sitting my sister's place. She's away for a few days."

"Oh," I said, relieved. "Does Gaz mind?"

"No, he's good with it. I have to sit my sister's house a lot. I like the independence of it. She has a boyfriend up in Sheffield and spends a lot of time there. Gaz occasionally stays the evening when he's not working, which isn't often," she added.

"He's working tonight then?"

"Yeah, he always works Thursdays. It's a good club. I'll have to take you there one day."

"I'm not sure I'd get in," I joked.

We arrived at Kez's sister's place after a short bus ride. It wasn't a very big flat and again in a rough-looking area, but inside was nicely decorated.

"What does your sister do?" I asked.

"She's on the social, but does bits and pieces of work here and there. She does cleaning work sometimes, cash in hand and I think her boyfriend bungs here a few quid now and then.

"Why doesn't she move to Sheffield?"

"Don't know. I've thought the same thing. Maybe because she's got too many friends and family down here."

Kez made us some vodka and Cokes before she got the pasta underway. This was the only alcohol she could find in the house. This made me wonder whether she'd intended on inviting me back at the start of the night. I suspected not. If I wanted to impress someone, I'd get something better in than pasta, washed down with vodka and Coke. I was also perplexed by the fact that she stayed in her sister's place when she was away. It didn't really need looking after. There weren't even any pets to feed or clean up after. I didn't mention this though.

We sat eating our pasta, talking about insubstantial subjects that seemed to crop up after a few drinks. Kez was generous with her vodka measurements and along with the beers in the pub I started to feel the effects of the alcohol. We ate at the small breakfast bar that was in her sister's kitchen. In the background, Kez had put on some music, the artist of which I didn't recognise. It was quite dancey, which wasn't really my thing.

We remained sitting in the kitchen even when we'd finished our pasta. It was getting late, too late for me to go home. I wondered where I'd be sleeping the night.

"So," Kez said inquisitively after a lull in our conversation. "I've been very good tonight and not asked you yet. Are you going to tell me about the gun now?"

My first feeling upon hearing this question was disappointment. I'd obviously have to decide how I was going to answer it, but Kez having asked the question brought back the possibility or reality that the only reason she'd invited me back here was because she still wanted to know my story behind the gun. The rest of the night and the previous night, including the kiss, had all been a ruse in a quest to find out one little bit of information. It was strange to think that she'd go to such lengths to find out something that I wouldn't have thought would matter to her.

In my drunken state, I was tempted to let it all out and tell her everything, but I knew I shouldn't. I also wanted to see her reaction to me not telling her. This might let me know if there was any other reason for me being here.

"I don't think I can tell you, Kez," I said.

"Why won't you tell me? Is it because you can't trust me with whatever the answer is?" It was obvious that this angered her, even though she was trying to seem calm externally.

"No, but—" I hesitated, trying to find the right words. "It's quite heavy. I really don't think I can let you know," I finished, not very happy with the way I expressed it. Kez sighed.

"If it's because you've killed someone, then you needn't worry about what I'd do or think. Gaz's gang distribute drugs to people that probably harm or kill people. I'm sure in his line of work he's regularly harming or even killing to make his business successful. I've got enough information to be a major police informant. I'm hardly going to shop you in for whatever it is you've done or going to do with that gun."

"I know. It's not that I'm worried about. I don't know, it's just I hardly know you."

Kez got up and went out the room without saying anything. I wondered if I'd pissed her off with my last comment. I was half expecting to get my marching orders.

She came back a couple of minutes later and put the empty plates of pasta in the sink. She'd placed items in front of her that suggested she was about to make a joint.

"You probably think it's really strange me wanting to know

about you and the gun. It's just that, as I've said before, you don't seem the sort of person and the whole thing intrigues me. Normally I like to think I can work a person out quickly, but I can't read you so I want you to tell me. I'm also used to people telling me what I want to know."

"I bet you are," I joked, although she didn't laugh at this.

Instead, she started transferring the tobacco from a cigarette into the small piece of paper normally used for roll-up cigarettes. Once complete, she placed it down on the surface top.

I watched as she then took the lump of pot and held it over a lighter flame. Gradually the substance crumbled at the bottom and she sprinkled it over the tobacco. She must have done this many times before; she appeared an expert. I wondered if her rolling this joint was in anyway related to the conversation we were having. Maybe her plan was to get me stoned in order to talk more.

"It's nothing personal why I'm not telling you. In fact, nobody knows." She looked up from what she was doing when I said this.

"That sounds like a burden," she said. She returned to her little job, rolling the joint slowly but perfectly. It gave the impression that it was not just the effects of the joint that she enjoyed, but also the task of creating it. I didn't respond to her last comment immediately. Instead, I continued to watch her as she finished her work by inserting a ready to fit bit of cardboard in the end of the joint where a filter would be on a cigarette. After turning it around between her fingers and inspecting it carefully, she eventually used the cigarette lighter to change it to its state of purpose. She took a large draw, holding down the smoke a long time before she exhaled.

"Are you offended?" I asked.

"I am a bit," she replied, after a short pause with her eyes closed, likely savouring the effects the joint was having.

I was thinking how to respond and how I could persuade her it wasn't personal when she spoke again.

"If you don't want to tell me, then that's OK, I understand." This made me feel a bit better, but I felt that there was a childish element to it. It was as if she was accepting it reluctantly and going to sulk about it. But then as if through a peace offering, she handed me the joint. I inhaled a lung full of smoke and looked up at Kez. At that moment, I couldn't believe I was there with her drinking, smoking, and chatting. I didn't want to ruin it; I could have happily stayed there for days.

"OK, I'll tell you." I couldn't believe I'd just come out with it. Although I could have backtracked, I felt I was committed now. A smile came over Kez's face. She looked pleased with herself, as though she'd achieved her aim. However, she seemed to be holding it back a little, as though she knew she'd not won until I told her.

"I'm a hit man," I said. She broke into spontaneous laughter. I knew she would somehow, especially given the alcohol and now cannabis intake she'd had. She set me off too and we both sat there laughing. I wasn't sure whether she was laughing because she didn't believe me or just at the idea of it. I didn't care really. Eventually she stopped.

"You're a what?"

"A hit man, an assassin," I giggled. The smoke had had an immediate effect on us. Kez laughed some more.

"You're not serious, are you?" Hearing this gave me a pang of regret. She wanted to ridicule me. I pulled a serious face. Although, I found this difficult even though I wanted to be serious.

"I'm serious, it's true."

"How many people have you killed?"

"Only two, I'm new to it."

This started her laughing again, which also set me off. Once we'd calmed back down, she spoke.

"You're serious, aren't you?"

"It's not the sort of thing you lie about."

"No, it's not." Her face twisted. She obviously had many questions on her mind. Before she spoke again, I started to relay my story. I told her everything from the moment I'd spoken to H in the pub until the last murder. I described my emotions at the time and my reasons for going through with it. She interrupted regularly, questioning, asking for clarification. I could see she was taking it all in, amazed at what she was hearing. Even when I stopped, she remained seated, silent, digesting all I had said.

"Well, I've got to admit, I'd have never of thought you had it in you." At this she started to roll another joint.

"So, do you have a problem with it then?" I asked.

"No. It's fine by me," she said matter-of-factly. Even though this was the answer I wanted to hear, it was weird. Now she had taken it all in, it seemed a small, almost insignificant subject. What sort of a person would react to this sort of story in such a way? However, I put this to the back of my mind and spoke to her.

"Actually, there's something you can help me with," I told her.

Kez looked up from what she was doing. "Yeah? What's that?"

"I need a silencer."

"A what?"

"A silencer, for my gun," I clarified.

This started her laughing again. "You're not in Hollywood," she joked.

"No, I do. I'm serious. It'll make it better for the next time."

Once she stopped laughing, she spoke. "What do you want me to do about it?"

"Ask Gaz, see if he can get me one."

"Not sure if I can do that. Like I told you, I don't get involved in his business, and anyway he'll want to know why."

"I know, but I don't know where else to go."

"Why don't you go through Jason like you did last time?" she suggested.

"I don't know. I'd rather not deal with him directly if I can help it. There's something about it I don't like." This time it was my turn to look sulky as I finished speaking. I could see Kez was thinking as she put the finishing touches to the joint.

"I'm not sure I can help you. I think you might have to go through Jason," she said. "He's nothing to be scared of, you know," she added.

I left the subject there, but I wasn't happy. I knew what Kez had said made sense. I imagined she would get questioned by Gaz if she asked him about it. She would have to come up with some elaborate lie and then it might get her into trouble or even put Gaz onto Kez and I. She was also right in that I was a bit scared of going through Jason. Getting her to do it was the easy option. I'd have to face my fears. Kez and I talked some more whilst we finished off another vodka and Coke and smoked a second joint she'd rolled. There was a break in the conversation as Kez looked at the clock on the oven.

"It's getting late," she said. "Do you want to stay here?" My heart beat faster as she said this.

"Yes, if that's OK." Kez didn't reply, she just smiled at me.

The next morning, we were woken up by the phone. There was one next to the bed on the side I was sleeping. Kez leaned over and answered it. I was still very tired. I kept my eyes shut but remained semi-conscious. I realised that the cocktail of drugs and booze would make me feel like staying in bed the whole day. Even though I was falling in and out of sleep as Kez talked, I could hear some of the conversation. She was different to whoever she was talking to. She seemed more subservient, agreeing to whatever was being said and taking orders. I heard her say that she stayed in and watched television last night. Then finally she said, "I'll be there as soon as possible." She put the phone down.

"You've got to get up," she said to me. I didn't want this. I could have quite happily stayed in bed with Kez all day. I reluctantly got out of bed after Kez had had a shower. She was clearly in a rush to leave and I wasn't offered a drink or breakfast. We left the house together.

"I'd offer you a lift, but I've got to run," she said. She kissed me quickly and left me standing there, a little dazed. I made my way home. Part of me was really buoyed by the evening I'd had with Kez. After I'd told her about my work, I'd not regretted it. However, this, morning I felt different. The way she rushed off and also how she'd been with me, quite cold and as though nothing had happened between us, worried me. It was obvious that she was rushing off to see Gaz. She hadn't even stopped to arrange another time to see me.

I got home and went back to bed. Later that day, when I finally got up, I opened my post and saw my lorry driving course and first test for had come through. It was in a couple of weeks' time. Over the next few days, I looked forward to it. I'd been bored, and I needed something to do. The sooner I could get myself some work the better.

As the days went by, I started to give up on Kez calling again. I wasn't sure if I should call her, but so far, she'd made all the running. It occurred to me that maybe now she'd found out about me and my reasons for buying the gun, she wasn't interested in seeing me again. If that was the case, she was stranger and shallower than I'd originally thought.

Contacting Jason occupied my thoughts regularly. I knew I had to do it and I was trying to build up the courage to do so. It was easy to put off, but I wanted to do it before I got my next envelope through. I needed to be prepared. I set myself a deadline by the end of next week, which I knew was just a way of delaying having to do it. However, before this time arrived, Kez called. I was at home on a Sunday night watching television. It had been ten days since I'd last seen her. I made a brief reference to this which she ignored. She asked if I wanted to meet up that night. I certainly had nothing better to do and therefore accepted her offer. We agreed to meet in the same pub as we'd met last time.

I readied myself straight away and made my way there, having agreed to meet within the hour. I thought about my relationship with Kez on the way. In one way, I liked it, as it was casual and easy and very unpredictable, but then she was making all the running. She decided when we'd go out and where. Also, she had another boyfriend. I didn't even think about this at first as it was a real buzz to be with her, but now I didn't like to think that she spent all her time with him. The fact that she hadn't even called me over the last ten days annoyed me. She could have spoken to me even if she wasn't able to meet me. On the other hand, and to be fair to Kez, she hadn't lied to me about anything. I'd known from the outset that she had a boyfriend. Therefore, I couldn't really complain. I was conscious I shouldn't get too involved, but I decided that I'd just carry on as normal for now. I could call it a day later if I became unhappy with how it was going. It wasn't worth the hassle of having arguments with her; that wasn't the type of relationship I wanted.

When I got to the pub she wasn't there. I got myself a drink and sat in the corner near to where we'd sat before. I waited there with a cigarette in one hand and a pint in the other, wondering what the night would hold.

When Kez walked in a little while later, I was reminded of why I was in no hurry to stop seeing her. She had a natural beauty that meant she didn't even need to make an effort to look attractive. She was casually dressed in a woolly jumper and black jeans. She had a little make up on around her eyes, but she'd hardly plastered it on. Her hair was tied neatly into a ponytail. She looked over to where I was and smiled as she made her way to the table I was sat at. I was instantly a happier person.

"Hi. Do you want me to get you a drink?" she said. I looked at my half empty pint.

"Hmm, yes please. Another one of these," I asked, holding up the glass.

She walked off to the bar. What I liked about Kez was that for some reason she made me feel like I didn't have to impress her. I could be my normal self with her. With any other girl I'd been with, I'd found I'd constantly felt the need to make an effort, to be on my best behaviour, whereas Kez seemed to accept who I was; there was no pretense. The bonus was, given her looks, I would have thought I'd have to ty to impress her every second I spent with her.

When Kez returned form the bar we started chatting as normal. We seemed to be able to talk easily. When I thought about what we should talk about before I met her, I couldn't think of anything; we didn't have any mutual friends, or shared experiences. However, there were no awkward silences and the conversation flowed naturally. There was nothing to suggest that it had been a while since we'd last met and she made no mention of this. She also hadn't discussed what I'd told her in her sister's kitchen the last time we saw each other. It was as though she'd forgotten it.

We'd been there about an hour when she did change the subject from the trivia we'd been talking about

"By the way, I've got some good news for you."

"Have you, what is it?" I replied, intrigued.

"I think I can get you a silencer," she said in her first reference to what I'd told her before.

"That's great. I didn't think you were going to try," I said, extremely happy with this unexpected news.

"I wasn't, but then I felt sorry for you. You owe me big time though. I had to tell an elaborate lie to get Gaz to look into it."

"What exactly is he going to get me?" I asked.

"Well, he asked me whether you wanted a silencer, or a gun that came with a silencer."

I was about to tell Kez that I wasn't sure how it worked, when she continued.

"So, I asked him if you could attach a silencer to any old handgun, as I figured you were an amateur in this and wouldn't know."

I laughed and said, "You were right."

"He said no. You have to do something with the barrel. Extend it or get a new barrel maybe. Anyway, I think it's easier to do with some makes than others. So, I took the executive decision to say you wanted a new gun, complete with silencer. He said he'd look into it."

"Cheers," I said. "That's excellent news. I definitely owe you one. Did he say how much it would cost?"

"No. He's not certain he can get one yet. He says he needs to check it out first."

"What did you tell him?"

"Oh, I gave him a sob story about a friend of a friend whose got themselves into a little bit of trouble and was worried that someone was going to take them out. It got tricky when he asked me where we could meet them."

"What did you say?"

"I said they were a bit worried about being out and about at the moment and that they'd prefer to only go through me. He accepted it, but he's a little suspicious to say the least. He asked why this person needed a silencer. I told him I had no idea. Anyway, I'm sure it'll work out all right."

"I hope so. Thanks again," I replied. She didn't seem convinced in her last statement. For the first time I thought I detected a small bit of fear in her. Up until now, she'd always come across as such a confident person. I was also concerned that she'd asked Gaz, even though I'd originally requested her to do so. It was a way he could find out about me and Kez. It also made me feel a bit of a coward, getting Kez to do my dirty work. After all I'd been through, I was disappointed in myself that I hadn't had the bottle to go through Jason.

We didn't talk about the subject afterwards. We kept chatting though until closing time. I'd kind of presumed we'd be heading back to Kez's sister's place afterwards, so I was disappointed when she said she had to go back home instead. With the way she'd said it, I hadn't asked if she wanted company. I knew that either Gaz would be there or she didn't want me coming back.

"So," I said as we stood outside the pub ready to go our

separate ways home, "when can I expect to hear from you again?" She looked pensive, as though genuinely thinking about when she could call me again. She obviously hadn't given it any prior thought.

"I'm not sure umm..."

"Within the next ten days?" I asked.

She looked confused initially, but then said, "Was that how long it was last time?"

"Yes."

"Oh, it didn't seem that long. I'll try to ring before that this time. OK?"

"Yes," I said, trying to hide my disappointment that she couldn't commit to more. Although I was down about this, the fact that she'd gone to a big effort to try to get me the gun was a big positive. If she didn't like me, she wouldn't have done that. It was something to cling to.

With a quick kiss on the lips she was gone, off into the night. I stood where she'd left me for a moment. When I was with her, it was as though I entered a different world. I felt as though I had an entirely separate existence that had no bearing on my real life. I could almost have mistaken my encounters with her as dreams. Only when she left did I return to the real world.

The next few days, I occupied myself with my first lorry driving course and test. There were three days of learning followed by the test. I enjoyed it because it was the first time in a while I had something to get my teeth into. It made me look forward to when I could start doing it as a job. I successfully passed and then booked the following course and test that would allow me to drive articulated lorries. This was also good from a money point of view, as although I still had a lot of cash from my dirty work, I was getting through it faster than I'd anticipated.

The security of earning would be better in case the assignments dried up.

Kez phoned me that Friday. She'd kept her promise to get in touch with me quicker this time. However, she was blunt and to the point. "Sorry, I've got to be quick. Can we meet up briefly on Sunday?" she said.

"Sure. Where and what time?" I replied.

"At my sister's place. Three o'clock."

"Three o'clock?" I said, thinking that was a strange time. "Are you cooking me Sunday lunch?" I joked.

"No, I've got your gun. Bring eight hundred quid, cash." She said very seriously, ignoring my light heartedness.

"Sure."

"See you then," she said, and I heard the click of the call being ended before I'd even removed the phone from my ear. I looked into the phone, slightly stunned by our conversation. The good news was she'd come up trumps with the gun and at a cut down price compared to my first purchase. I wasn't sure how she'd achieved it, but I wasn't going to complain. Going through Kez was good from that respect. It probably meant I'd been ripped off by Jason.

Given Kez's tone and manner on the phone, I didn't expect our liaison on that Sunday to be long and I wasn't proved to be wrong. I made sure I was on time and was if anything knocking on the door a few minutes early. Kez let me in without saying anything. She pointed me through to the living room. I sat down on an armchair that was positioned opposite the switched off television.

"Your sister not in?" I said, trying to make conversation as the atmosphere felt different to when I normally saw Kez.

"No, but she'll be back soon, so we had better be quick,"

Kez replied. She picked up a box from the table and handed it to me. It was a brown, made of cardboard and about the size of a shoe box.

"Everything you need is in there," she said. She seemed stressed, not her normal calm self. It made me nervous.

"Have you got the money?"

"Yes," I said and pulled out a roll of notes from my pocket that I'd previously counted.

"It's all there," I said. It felt weird, as this seemed like a formal business meeting, rather than two people getting together who'd been intimate with each other. I sensed Kez wanted me to leave as soon as possible. "Thanks a lot, I really appreciate you doing this."

"You should," she responded. "I had to lie my arse off to get it."

"Sorry. I owe you one. How come it's so cheap?" I asked.

"Cheap?" She replied.

"Yes. My last one cost twelve hundred quid."

"It's probably nearer cost price, because it's me." She said without much thought. I reckoned she was right. Jason had taken me for a few quid the first time round. That was for sure.

"Look, I've got to go," Kez said.

"OK." I knew that Kez could be a very cold person at times, but today she'd hit a peak. I was concerned that she had a problem with me. As we walked towards the front door, I voiced my concern.

"You OK today, Kez? You seem a little stressed."

She turned to me and smiled. "I'm just busy and in a rush," she said.

"So, we are all good then?" I asked.

"Of course," she replied in a manner that indicated she

thought I was being daft. It made me feel better for a moment, although this was overridden with a sense of disappointment that our meeting was ending so soon, even if I'd expected it.

We got outside and she looked like she was going to rush off without saying goodbye.

"Kez," I called. "Can I expect you to call again?" I regretted asking this almost immediately. It indicated a weakness and also highlighted to Kez I really wanted to see her again. As though I had a big fear she wasn't going to call anymore, which annoyingly, I did.

"Yes, of course," she replied without hesitating. "Although, I'm off to Spain for a couple of weeks tomorrow. So, when I'm back maybe.

"Spain?" I questioned. More just confirming it to myself then asking her to clarify it.

"Yes. Look, I'll see you later. Take care with that thing," she said, diverting her eyes to the box I was holding. With that she took off, almost at running speed.

I walked back to the car, thinking over the brief encounter we'd just had. It had been strange to say the least. There hadn't been any physical contact between us. I thought it didn't bode well for our relationship going forward. I'd be better off not bothering with her anymore. It could turn out to be more trouble than it's worth.

I got into my car and put the box on the passenger seat. I hadn't even checked the contents of it yet. There could be anything in there. However, upon my return home, I looked inside to see Kez had indeed brought me the gun. It looked impressive, although I had no idea whether it was a good one or not. I should have used the free time I'd had over the past few weeks to do a bit more research on guns. It concerned me I wasn't professional enough at times to carry on doing what I did without messing up and being caught. I imagined most professional hit men had trained up somewhere like the army and knew their stuff about ballistics. I had no history with guns whatsoever. However, I'd succeeded before and I told myself I had to believe and have the confidence I could carry on doing it.

Chapter Seven

As if by strange coincidence, there was an envelope in my box at the post office later that week. I saw it as a good sign now that I'd got myself sorted with the gun I wanted. It didn't stop my nerves starting up again though. This time though, I felt a buzz, not just created by nerves, but also by excitement. I was going away on a mission and into the unknown once more. I did my usual routine of taking the envelope home before opening it.

John Wheeler, aged thirty-eight, lived in a village just outside Leeds. He was five foot eight inches tall, weighed twelve stone and was balding. The financial terms were exactly the same as my last job. However, this time, there was an added pressure, as, unlike my first two jobs, this one had a deadline. I had fifteen days to kill this man, otherwise I would not get my completion payment. This meant that if I didn't do it in the allotted time, it was hardly worth doing at all. I sat in my flat, wondering why there was a deadline. What was this guy going to do after that time that made someone want him dead? They were making my work more difficult with each hit. Firstly, there was the deadline which meant I had to move fast and plan quickly. This was greater pressure. Also, this guy lived in a village, which meant I was more likely to stand out and be potentially noticed as a stranger. To me, it meant the payment should be higher.

However, I was hardly in a position to negotiate or complain, given that I didn't have a clue who I was taking my instructions from. I could always try to find them, but I knew this would be difficult, on top of the fact that I was certain they wouldn't receive my suggestions well. I had to admit that I was a little frightened of these people, whoever they were, and even if I had the means to contact them, I'm not sure I would complain about something like this.

I wanted to get up north as soon as possible to allow myself as much time to do my work. There was one thing I wanted to do first though. I felt that it was time to change my car. This was partly down to paranoia. I worried that if the police were to link the murders, somehow my car may crop up as being in each of the areas. I realised that even if I got a new car, it would be registered in my name and therefore traceable to me, but somehow it felt more secure. I also had the money to upgrade a little as well. Not having the time to look around extensively for something good or bargain for a decent deal, I went to a local dealer and picked up something marginally better. I knew a little about cars; my dad was a reasonable mechanic and had taught me about it whilst I was growing up. So, I had the confidence to know what to look for to ensure I didn't get ripped off. Having said that, I had got a poor price for my car, although I had expected this. It was car dealer's business to do so.

I took to the road that weekend in my newly acquired car and headed up north. I checked myself into a hotel in Leeds under a false name, as I'd done the last two times. I didn't want to stay in the village where John Wheeler lived because of the worry I'd stand out. Staying in a big city, like Leeds, would make me more inconspicuous. I liked being away on a job. I had nobody to answer to and felt a free spirit. Admittedly, the idea of killing someone still scared me, but that added to the excitement and the adventure.

The next day I drove over to the village where John lived.

His home was what looked like a small flat above a newsagent's shop. I hung around a while that morning which was easier to do without looking too suspicious, given that it was a busy Saturday. I thought about the process of waiting around outside people's homes. It would be much more helpful if I was provided a place of work as well what their typical movements were. It would make life much easier and more risk adverse. This was another comment I was unable to pass onto my employees.

Conveniently, there was a coffee shop across the road that gave me a good vantage point of the door that led to his flat. So, feeling like a true spy, I sat there with a cup of coffee and newspaper and waited. As time went by, I was regretting my late start that morning. I wondered if he'd gone out before I got there, my thinking being that he probably wouldn't be up and about early as it was a Saturday. But then I didn't know anything about him, so it was quite an assumption to make. And anyway, he might still be in the flat.

I ended up having a snack for lunch as time got on, staying in the café watching as much as possible. Eventually my patience paid off and I saw him return to his flat at around quarter past two. I stayed around for a bit longer to see if he went out again, but there was no movement. After that, I went to investigate the rear of his flat. There was a car park around the back of the shops that was private for residents and shop workers. I could see what I thought was the back of his flat from there. I was becoming confident that he lived on his own. It was possible he might share the flat with a partner, but it looked to me to be only big enough for one bedroom and therefore unlikely he had children or a flat mate. I noticed that he had a balcony at the back and a door leading onto it. Next to the balcony, but not adjoining were a set of stairs that looked like a fire escape from the adjacent building.

There was a gap of about a metre between the stairs and John's balcony. I reckoned I could jump across it quite easily.

The plan I had was that, given he probably lived on his own, I could wait until he was out, break into his flat and lie in wait for him. Killing him in his flat would be perfect from the point of view of not having to worry about being seen. Also, now I had a silencer, nobody would be alerted by the noise of a gun going off. So, in theory the plan seemed sound. First, however, I had to establish for definite whether he did live on his own, as my plan depended on this. At the same time, I needed to see if he had a daily routine of going to work. Ideally, it would be better to break in at a quieter time of the day, but his movements would solely dictate this. Whilst thinking of all this, I was conscious of my deadline. If, for whatever reason, my plan wasn't feasible, I needed to know sooner rather than later so I could put together an alternative one quickly.

Despite my need to move quickly, I decided I didn't have much to gain by going there on Sunday. It would be likely his comings and goings wouldn't be consistent with the rest of the week. I didn't want to loiter in the village more than necessary. Even though I'd tried to change my appearance as much as possible, the more I hung around the village and was seen, the more chance I had of becoming a suspect afterwards. So, instead I decided to do my next surveillance on Monday morning.

I made sure I got there just before half past seven so I could catch him if he left his flat early. However, having hung around for a couple of hours, nobody came or went from the front door. I felt uncomfortable loitering around so much. I therefore decided to leave the village and return a little later. I went back to Leeds and found somewhere to eat. I was cursing my luck. It was possible that he'd left earlier than I'd arrived, but in all probability, he hadn't left at all.

If he was unemployed or without a routine, my plan would be thwarted. I felt aggrieved as this was the second person I'd been assigned who didn't seem to have regular movements or a job.

I went back to the village later in the afternoon to try my luck again. This time things went my way and I saw him return to his flat at around the same time he did on Saturday. Maybe I'd been wrong about him being out of work. Perhaps he did early shifts somewhere and worked Saturdays. He could be something like a postman. I thought that it would be worth my while to monitor his flat very early the next morning. This way I could catch him if he did, in fact, leave early. So, I returned to my hotel ready to carry out my plan the next day.

Spending lonely nights in a basic hotel room didn't bother me as much as I thought it would. I wouldn't say I was a natural loner; in fact, I'd always surrounded myself with friends. However, going away made me realise that I liked my own company. I had much more time to think. I even read, something I rarely did before. The only person I thought about whilst up in Leeds was Kez. I did miss her company and the buzz of being around her. I wondered what she was up to in Spain, whether it was a business trip for Gaz, and she was accompanying him, or if they were on a romantic holiday together. It was even possible she'd gone with friends; I didn't know. She'd been gone a week now and would be back next week. I wondered if she'd contact me when she returned.

I knew though, that I needed to straighten my mind on her. I wanted to be independent and not rely on her. I didn't want to be committed to anyone, on top of the fact I didn't think our relationship would last for long. The last thing I wanted to be was lovesick. I'd been down that road recently enough.

So, despite having lots of time to myself, I didn't feel bored. I even explored Leeds a little and took an interest in it. As a southerner, I'd underestimated it. It had a better feel to it than I'd expected.

The next morning, I was up extremely early. I arrived at the village at a little after five. It was still very dark at this point and the village was dead, with nobody around. This made it easy to sit in my car, which I'd parked so that I could see his front door, safe in the knowledge that nobody was watching me. I found it difficult to stay awake, but around half an hour later my efforts were rewarded when John appeared and left his flat. My plan had worked. He walked around to the back of the shops to where the car park was. Within a minute, a car appeared with John behind the wheel. I ducked down in my car as he drove past. I then started after him. I was concerned he might notice that someone was following him, as there was very little traffic on the road. However, I wanted to take a chance on this as I felt it important to know what his job was and that it was a place of work he was going to. This way, if I broke into his flat, I could be certain he'd be out. We only drove a short way before he turned off the main road and into a supermarket. It was just before a town that was next along from his village.

He parked near the entrance of the supermarket. I wondered what he was doing. Did he work here, or did he want to buy something? I didn't think it was open yet. I hung back and watched him. He got out and looked over to where I'd parked which quickened the beating of my heart. As quickly as he looked over, he turned away and then walked into a side entrance to the shop. When he'd disappeared, I got out and checked the opening times. It wasn't due to open up until eight. I wondered what he did until that time. Perhaps he was a shelf packer. I drove away and went into the nearby town for breakfast.

I had a curiosity to find out exactly what he did in the supermarket. I therefore decided to go back a little later. Another thing I wanted to check was that he returned to his flat at around the same time I'd seen him on Saturday and Monday. If this happened, then I'd be fully aware of his routine.

I returned to the supermarket a few hours later to see if I could spot him. I knew I was taking a little risk, but then he wouldn't know who I was. He wouldn't have seen me earlier this morning, despite seeing my car. I walked around the supermarket, pretending to be shopping, putting a few things in a basket. It took me a while to find him, but eventually I spotted him bringing out some fresh bread behind the bakery counter. I moved away quickly, before he noticed me, happy that I'd seen him. It all fell into place. He was a baker and that was therefore the requirement for him to start early.

I went back to my car and drove off, happy that I'd made progress. At two o'clock I was back in the village and waiting for his return. Sure enough, he showed up as normal at quarter past two and went inside his flat. I returned to my hotel for the remainder of the day. My biggest job now was to psyche myself up for the next day. My main worry about my whole plan was how I was going to get into his flat. I knew I could get onto his balcony, but getting inside would be a different prospect. If I couldn't, I was in trouble. I didn't have many backup plans either. I could maybe get a chance to take him out at the supermarket, first thing in the morning. It was quiet at that time. I could also wait for him in the car park behind the shops where he lived. These were more high-risk plans than waiting for him in his flat, as I could be spotted despite the time of day. Therefore, breaking into his flat was my priority.

The next morning was, once more, a very early start. However, whereas yesterday I'd had that dazed feeling I get when I wake up early, this time I felt more alive and alert. Surprisingly I'd slept well, which meant tiredness wasn't able to suppress my lively feeling. I drove there with a pang of excitement in my stomach. I wasn't nervous, like I'd thought I might be. I parked in a different place this time. Instead of parking near to the shops, I drove into the car park, which was set off the main road at one end of the high street. I walked the short walk to where John's flat was and sheltered in one of the shop's entrances across the road. It was still dark, and it was unlikely he'd notice me if I kept still and quiet. Almost to the minute he appeared at his door and walked around to the car park. He didn't look over at all in my direction. Shortly afterwards he was driving away. I waited a few minutes, having a fag outside the shop door. Then I walked across the road and around to the car park. I climbed the stairs of the adjacent building. Once near to John's balcony, I climbed up onto the rail of the stairs. It was a bit of a jump and looked worse from higher up. I knew I could make it, though. I took the leap and landed on top of the rail of the balcony of the flat. I slipped as I did this, but fortunately fell forwards, my momentum taking me this way. I landed on the floor of the balcony on my hands and knees. Fortunately, I was unhurt. There were some fag butts littering the area I'd fallen onto; it also smelt of smoke. As I saw this, I wondered what the guy had done. Why was someone willing to have him killed? It was an intrigue I'd had with all the people I'd been assigned so far. None of them had obvious problems or issues that seemed serious enough to get them into this much trouble. Admittedly, I'd not got to know any of them that well, but even so, I'd have expected something to stand out as a reason why. It just added to the mystery of what I was being paid to do and the set up behind it.

I looked at the door that led onto the balcony. The top half of it was glass, the bottom a wooden panel. To the right was a window with a large enough gap to get through should I be able to get it open. I tried the handle of the back door with my gloved hand without even thinking. Amazingly, as I turned and pushed the door gave way and opened. I couldn't believe it was as simple as that. Surely, he was more security conscious. Maybe he had no idea that there was someone out there after him or was just absent-minded. Still, it seemed too easy; something told me all was not right. However, this did not deter me. As I entered the door, I found myself in a dark room. I looked around, waiting for my eyes to adjust. I could make out that it was a kitchen. I fumbled for the light as I shut the back door. I located it and turned it on. The kitchen was small and compact. All spare space was used with cupboards and racks. The door opposite me led into a corridor and the rest of the flat. The corridor had other doorways leading from it. The kitchen was poorly decorated and maintained. The appliances seemed old and had stains on them. The small amount of visible wall had paint on it that was cracking and peeling. A discoloured linoleum formed the flooring. John Wheeler clearly wasn't very good at keeping it clean and tidy, not that I was one to talk when it came to cleaning. I decided to explore the other rooms when something stopped me in my tracks. I noticed in the corridor a pair of women's shoes. I felt sick all of a sudden. Surely, he didn't live here with someone. But if he lived on his own, why would a pair of women's shoes be in his flat? I stood there, statue-like, mulling over in my head what my next move should be. I hadn't seen anyone other than him leave or enter the flat during my observations. But then I'd hardly done extensive surveillance of the flat. Also, it may be that the shoes belonged to a girlfriend who occasionally stayed over. It didn't add up somehow. I had to make a decision. Did I get out now, which was my instinct, or did I stay and find out if someone was really in the flat? The first option seemed the most sensible, but I was held back by the thought of how I'd execute my mission if I gave up on this plan. It wouldn't be easy, given my deadline, and therefore I decided I should find out for definite if the flat was occupied or not.

I turned around, walked to the back door and turned off the light. I decided I'd creep back to the corridor and listen for noises. Chances were that if there was anyone in the flat, they'd be asleep. Otherwise, they probably would have heard me come in. I waited a minute by the back door before moving so my eyes adjusted better to the darkness. There was a glint of light coming in through the window, but not much. I tiptoed back to the corridor and looked at the doors. There were three, all to the left. Two were shut and the one opposite the front door, which was to the far right, was slightly ajar. I moved forward to it and poked my head around. I could make out a living area. I moved back to the other doors. One must be a bathroom, the other a bedroom. I guessed that the bathroom was likely to be nearer to the kitchen. I tried the door first, slowly turning the handle. I could make out a silhouette of a toilet and sink. Nothing there. That left the bedroom: the most likely place the girl would be if she was here.

I breathed in deeply and turned the handle. I peered around the door; the room was dark. I stayed still, hoping my eyes would adjust so I could see the bed. Suddenly I saw and heard movement of what appeared to be a duvet. Then someone spoke.

"Is that you, John?" Panic and a sickening feeling hit me.

Quickly, I closed the door and moved fast back to the kitchen. I opened the back door and went out onto the balcony, closing it behind me. I then climbed back onto the balcony and jumped across to the stairs. I ran down them and away through the car park, not looking back to see if the girl had followed me out. Quickly getting into my car, I drove back to Leeds.

Back in my hotel, I felt frustration and disappointment that I'd failed. It had been a big anti-climax. I'd now have to implement a plan B. I would lie in wait for him in the car park.

Thinking about the morning's events, I realised just how much of a close shave I'd had. If the girl in the flat had been more alert or awake, I'd have been caught red-handed. Then what would I have done? If I ran, she'd alert John about me and then he'd have his wits about him. Shooting her would have been an option, but a big mess to clear up before John had got home. I was lucky I hadn't had to make the choice.

The episode had shaken me up a bit. Part of me wanted to pack it all in and drive back home. However, I knew this wasn't an option. The position I was in didn't grant me the choice. I sat in my hotel for the rest of the day, feeling depressed. I also beat myself up over what had happened. I shouldn't have been so rash and just burst into the flat without more thorough observation. I hadn't watched the place that much to know for certain that nobody else stayed there. If I was to be successful and survive in this business, I needed to be more professional.

I thought about carrying out my alternative plan the next morning, but I felt I needed the time to psyche myself up again for the task as well as rebuild my confidence. I decided I'd go back the morning after that.

The following twenty-four hours dragged like hell. I didn't know what to do with myself. I spent a lot of time wandering around, walking the streets of Leeds, thinking over what had happened and what I was about to do. I had to be successful this time. I couldn't fail again. I wondered if John's girlfriend had been awake enough to wonder who it was in the flat. She might have heard me go out the back door. Would she have spoken to John about it? Almost certainly if she felt it was suspicious. He might already be more on his guard because of this and they may have even reported it to the police.

The night before I was to try my second attempt, I hardly slept. My mind was racing. I had a sick feeling in my stomach. The anticipation of what was about to happen the next day was playing with me.

I was awake early and certainly not feeling tired despite my lack of sleep. As I drove to the village, it felt like a life defining moment was about to happen. Although I'd done it twice before and was now more comfortable with the idea of murdering someone, it was the fact that I'd already tried and failed on the first attempt, as well as almost being caught in the process that unnerved me. It had undoubtedly knocked me back. I needed to build up my confidence and the belief I could do it, which I was trying to instil in myself as I approached where he lived.

I parked my car in the same place as two days earlier. I was about twenty-five minutes early. I waited for a few moments before I got out of my car and made my way to where John's car was parked. He seemed to always park it at one end of the car park, near the steps that lead to the property next to his flat. There was an industrial-sized rubbish bin in the corner of the car park nearest to where his car had been left. I saw there was enough space behind it for me to squeeze in between it and the wall. I looked around before moving behind the bin to see if anybody was about. There was no one and there was also an eerie silence about the place. I moved behind it and crouched down. I positioned myself at the end of it furthest from the corner so I could peep around it regularly. By my calculations, John would be approaching his car in just over ten minutes.

There was about fifteen metres between where I was positioned and John's car. I would have to cover the ground quickly, as I didn't want to fire from where I was. I wasn't confident enough I'd hit him. I needed to be sharp. I wouldn't consider myself unfit but as I sat there, I realised I should get myself into good shape. I thought it likely that most hit men did. I peered down at the gun I was now clutching in sweaty palms. I'd never even fired it before. I couldn't even be sure it worked. Waiting there in the dark made me realise how much of a risk I was taking. It was too late to pull out now though; I was going ahead. As the moment of expectation of when he would appear came, I visualised my move. Wait for him to get to the driver's side of the car, which was the side nearer to me. Get close to him quickly and quietly and then drill a shot into his back, move to point blank range and fire one to the head. Then run like hell back to my car and return to my hotel.

I looked at my watch; it should be any moment now. As I looked up, sure enough, he was there approaching his car. All of a sudden, I felt really calm, and something told me everything was going to be OK. I was focused. Peering out from behind the bin, I studied John as he made his way to the car. He looked on automatic pilot, as you'd expect at that time of the morning. This was good as he seemed unaware of what was around him. I was chomping at the bit to make my move, but I knew I had to be patient and wait for the right moment. It soon came. He reached the driver's side of the car, turned his back and searched his pocket for the key. This was perfect. I leapt out from behind the bin, with the gun in my hand. I covered half the ground between us before quickly aiming the gun and firing. He had one hand on the door handle as I did this. He looked as though he was about to turn around, his senses detecting movement behind him. As the bullet hit him, just above the centre of his back, his body jolted as though he'd been given a large electric shock. I didn't really register it at the time, but thinking back afterwards, the noise from the gun was negligible and sounded cool. His body slumped forward, I closed the gap between us and put the gun to his head. I pulled the trigger once more. As soon as I'd done this, as I had envisaged beforehand, I ran back towards my car. It was still early and there was nobody around.

I reached my car in quick time and climbed straight into it, having left it unlocked. I waited a few seconds, catching my breath and calming myself for the drive. I felt good. Adrenaline, as with the last two times, was flowing fast, but I was on a high. It had gone perfectly, and I felt I'd carried it out professionally.

I drove back to Leeds in a calm manner, composed. I wanted to avoid driving fast and thereby possibly drawing attention to myself. This wasn't easy, as because of the way I was feeling, my instinct was to drive quickly.

I didn't return to my hotel straight away. Instead, I went into Leeds to get some breakfast. I didn't feel like eating, but then I thought it would be good for me. Before finding somewhere to eat, I got changed in a public toilet; once again I'd bought clothes especially for the job to give myself a new image. I'd also worn a balaclava for the assassination itself, but then taken it off as soon as I'd got back to my car. I waited in my car until half past seven. I then searched for an old-fashioned café that did a good fry-up.

I sat in the café with a mug of tea, chomping on some good

food, whilst reading the paper. I looked like everyone else in there, a normal start to the day. However, my work was already done. Life felt fine.

Just over twenty-four hours later, I was heading back towards London. During the drive, I reviewed this latest experience in my new life. I'd still been nervous beforehand and there was the blip when I was almost caught breaking into the flat. However, all had ended well. There were things I could have done better as well as things I needed to work on, such as fitness, but the job had been done and within time. In addition, I didn't have the paranoia or the worry that I'd gone through before. I certainly didn't feel guilty about what I'd done either. I was happy with the way I'd executed my task in the end and was already looking forward to the next one and experiencing the buzz again.

Once home, I sat down with a drink, feeling satisfied. The weekend was approaching and I thought about meeting up with my mates. Although, they'd probably be asking about where I was the last week. I found recently that I felt less inclined to see them. It was an occupational hazard. Whereas a few months back, before I'd met H and turned into a hit man, my whole life revolved around meeting my mates in the pub and getting drunk with them. Now things had changed. My new line of work had made me appreciate my own company more and to be less reliant on other people. I saw this as a good thing, as the more independent I was and less reliant on others, the better. The one person I did think about seeing was Kez. Although, I had little or no control over this. I was still having mixed thoughts over what I should do about her. Instinct told me I should forget about her and move on. The relationship had been based on her terms and I had been the one sitting by the phone waiting and hoping she'd call. The way she'd treated me so far, it was likely at some point she wouldn't call, and I felt the longer that I left the possibility of that happening, the worse I'd feel when it did occur. Also, in some ways I'd already got something good out of the relationship through the gun. However, I couldn't get around the fact that I was very much attracted to her, as well as that she intrigued me as a person. She had a habit of contacting me just as I'd given up on her and keeping me interested. I didn't know what her aim was for our relationship and that added to the intrigue. I knew deep down that I couldn't end it; I liked her too much. The best result would be for her not to call. That way it would prevent me from making a difficult decision.

It pleased me, when I thought about it, how little I'd been paranoid in the first few days since returning from Leeds. I'd managed to avoid any media regarding the murder and had not been too concerned about being caught. The police had no reason to suspect me in any of these murders as I wasn't previously connected with any of the people I'd killed. As long as nobody had seen me commit the crimes and I had left no trace, I was still a free man.

Being back home had concentrated my mind on my life without a real job once more. However, my second lorry driving course was less than two weeks away, so this was a goal. My life until then was quiet. I received the second payment for the job I'd done a week after I returned. It was always a relief getting paid, knowing I had no course of action to take should it not come through. Now that my stash of money was accumulating, I needed to think about what to do with it. I was still in a dilemma regarding openly spending it or investing it. I also didn't know the first thing about money laundering, which would become a necessity if jobs kept coming in. For the moment, my copious amount of bank notes were placed in various random hiding places in my flat. I figured that the more places I hid the money, the more chance I'd not lose it all should I get burgled. I wondered how other people, such as Jason, who came by money illegally, made it add up in the eyes of the tax man and the police. It was something I needed to read up on.

Chapter Eight

It was Sunday night, a week and a half after my return from Leeds, when Kez called. By my calculations, she'd been back nearly a week from Spain. Upon hearing her voice, I had mixed emotions. Part of me was excited to hear from her for the first time in a few weeks. It brought back vividly the feelings I had for her. On the other hand, over the last few days, I'd been thinking about her less and less. I began to feel I was achieving my aim of forgetting about her and moving on. Now, all that had been dashed. It was probably detectable to her, by the way I greeted her on the phone, that I was delighted she'd called, so there was no hiding it from myself. She asked me how I was, but then deflected my questions regarding her time in Spain and what she'd been up to. She once again was direct and to the point, asking me what I was doing on Wednesday afternoon. I told her that I had my lorry driving course booked for the week and therefore I wouldn't be around. She sounded exasperated by this, which annoyed me. Her tone was along the line of, can't you change it? I told her this wasn't possible and asked when else we could get together

"I'm not sure," she replied. "I'll call you back." She seemed annoyed and put out by everything, particularly when things weren't as she'd expected. She was a control freak if ever there was one, not ideal as a partner.

I huffed a goodbye. The phone call had annoyed me. She must take me for an idiot. She was obviously completely inflexible about when she could meet me. It made me think again what her motivations were and why she bothered to see me at all. I managed to put it to the back of my mind and calm myself down.

Thinking about it later once my annoyance had subsided, I realised that the phone call would, if anything, help me to stick to my original plan of forgetting about her.

As it happened, events over the next week assisted me in forgetting Kez. A casual visit to my mailbox at the post office on the Monday morning brought another envelope. I was amazed, as this was so soon coming after my last assignment. If they carried on coming like this, the population would start to diminish, and I'd be seriously rich. It was bad timing from my point of view, as I was due to start my three-day lorry course the next day. I scanned the instruction sheet paper to see if there was a deadline. Fortunately, there wasn't, so I thought I could set about my business at the end of the week. For the first time, the person who'd I'd been assigned to kill lived in London, just across town from me. I wasn't sure if I was happy about this. I'd liked the fact that my three previous hits had been far away from where I lived. The fact that this one was comparatively on my doorstep made me feel more vulnerable to being caught. It felt too close to home. I also felt that being away helped me focus on my job, with nothing to distract me. I was there for one reason only and it helped me obtain the right mindset.

Donovan Stephens was six foot two and weighed sixteen stone. He was twenty-six years of age. Coupled with his large physique was a look of someone you didn't want to be on the wrong side of: sharp features and an anger within his dark eyes. He looked and sounded a frightening prospect. Of course, I would be trying to shoot him, rather than fight him, but even so psychologically it was a tough assignment. I felt like they were becoming harder. If this was deliberate, it would mean that whoever controlled this operation had so many people they needed killing that they could match targets with assassins. On the other hand, I might have just got unlucky. However, the job must have been on my mind over the next few days, because at the end of my driving course I failed the test. This was annoying, but I knew it was down to the fact my mind was elsewhere.

That Friday, I ventured over to Donovan's place for the first time. The council estate he lived in was not dissimilar to where Jason lived. Donovan's flat was two stories up in a block that must have been ten high. There was a car park opposite where he would exit out onto from the stairs leading to his flat. I parked there to observe. It wasn't a pleasant area and I saw quite a few unsavoury characters whilst I watched for Donovan. The more I sat there, the more I felt that this was going to be a difficult assignment. I waited for a while and managed to see him leaving his flat. He was with two mates and they were obviously off out somewhere for the evening. I didn't follow as they were on foot. I didn't want to leave my car in that car park. I wasn't sure I could legally park it there, on top of the fact that I was concerned it would be stolen or vandalised within minutes of me walking off. In addition to this, I wasn't too bothered about following him as I couldn't believe I'd find an opportunity to take him out in this area. It was likely he wasn't going far and he'd always be with his mates, as well as in a built-up area.

Instead, I went up to where his flat was. I knocked on the door. I knew I was taking a risk, but I wanted to see if he lived with anyone. I already thought that the best way to get at him would be in his own place. If he lived on his own, which I hoped he did, this would be more feasible. Another thing that went in my favour was that his door looked as though it could be barged in quite easily. Nobody answered, which was positive. My thinking was that I could break in one night during the early hours of the morning. This way, even if I awoke him breaking in, I could get at him when he was unaware or dazed. He may also sleep through it if I was lucky. As usual, there were risks involved, not least him waking up and putting up a fight. Another thing was that there was only one escape route from his flat, as far as I could see. This was down the set of stairs I'd watched him come out from earlier. This made me feel vulnerable to being caught or seen escaping.

Over the course of the next few days, I monitored his flat. I saw him come and go regularly. He was often with friends, but it looked as though I was in luck. He didn't appear to live with anyone; I never saw him come and go with any girls and I saw him go back to his flat a couple of times on his own, late at night. I'd done quite a bit of loitering in the area during my observation times. I knew this was increasing my chances of being noticed and identified after I'd done the hit. However, I was working on the theory that because it was such a built up and busy area nobody would think twice of someone sitting around in a car and therefore not take proper note of it. I did decide, once I was satisfied that he lived on his own, that I would stay away for a few days. This might make anybody who had noticed me think it was unrelated to the crime I was about to commit.

A few days later I went back. This time, I parked a few streets away from his block of flats and made my way there on foot. I'd decided to make sure he went home alone that night, so I didn't have anybody other than him to deal with. He must have had a daytime job because I observed him regularly arriving back home around five in the evening. I therefore got there just before this time. I was lucky as he'd stuck to his normal pattern. I waited around, keeping an eye on his flat. I was sure he'd go out again as I'd seen him do so before. However, as time went on there was no sign of him leaving. I had to keep watching his door so that nobody else went in. It was a painful process of patience. But by late evening, there had been no coming or going and so I went back to my car to get some rest for a few hours before making a move.

I tried to get some sleep whilst I was there, but because of the things on my mind and some drunks banging on the window of my car it wasn't possible. I waited until three in the morning before I left the car. It was a Tuesday night which should mean it being quiet.

It was certainly that as I made the ten-minute walk over to where Donovan lived. This pleased me, but also gave off an eerie atmosphere which heightened my nerves. I was excited and looking forward to this task, given that I felt this was my biggest challenge so far. I was obviously nervous as well. Whereas, with my previous three killings, my main concern had been being caught, with this one, it was being overpowered and seriously hurt. I feared that if somehow he got the gun from me, he would beat me to a pulp. I also knew my plan was risky, as even though the front door seemed flimsy, it would still need a forcible shove to open it.

I made my way up the stairs to the floor of his flat and once again checked the gun I'd wedged down the back of my jeans. As I got to the top I stopped, looked around and listened. Again, I observed how quiet it was for a London suburb. The calm before the storm, I thought. I stayed still longer than necessary to confirm there wasn't anyone about. It was peaceful and I took the time to relax myself. It was a good opportunity to focus my mind on the job ahead. Visualise what I was going to do.

I took a few steps back and charged towards the door, left shoulder first. The impact hurt. I felt a shock of pain run through my shoulder and then across my collar bone and neck. It also made a loud noise that seemed to echo around the silent estate. The calm had been broken. I quickly assessed the damage to the door. It was still shut but I had made headway. The door seemed to have moved a little way inwards and the lock looked as though it was about to give. I stepped back and repeated my charge, although this time with my right shoulder. Once again, I felt pain upon impact. I also felt something give on the door. I quickly inspected it. The lock had completely broken away. However, the door hadn't fully opened and it was ajar instead. I gave it a firm push. It moved forward a little and then stopped. I couldn't push it further. I studied the lock area again, peering in the darkness. I saw what the problem was. There was a metal latch, a chain, which was preventing the door from completely opening. I couldn't believe he'd been so security conscious. Maybe he was expecting someone like me.

I stood, still staring at the door, frantic, thinking what I should do. In a few seconds, I went through my options. Run; try to shoot the latch open; break the glass panel in the door to allow me to unhook the latch; even kick in the wooden panel at the bottom of the door. None of these options seemed appealing, but, in a split-second decision, I decided I'd try to shoot the latch away. I aimed and fired immediately after I'd made my mind up. Somehow the latch stayed intact. Had I missed? I must have, even though I was at point blank range. I stared at it for a few seconds, realising my problems were growing, but telling myself not to panic. I held the gun up again ready to give it another go. But before I pulled the trigger, I heard a scream from inside. I'm not sure if the cry was meant to be a word or just a noise. To me, it was animal-like. I froze. What should I do? Suddenly a light came on from inside the flat. I saw a shadow appear behind the frosted glass of the battered front door. I ducked down and moved away from the door.

For a few seconds, I didn't detect any movement or sound form inside. I didn't know what to do. Would he come out after me? Maybe he was calling the police or for help. I didn't have to wait long for my answer. I heard him fiddling with the chain; he was coming after me. I couldn't believe how alert he was. Assuming he was asleep when I first started trying to bash down his door, he'd reacted very quickly. My immediate reaction to hearing him opening the door was one of fear, but then I realised this was a perfect opportunity. I quickly stood up and took a large stride back, holding my gun ready in position to fire. By the time I'd done this, he was poking his head out of the door. I needed him to step out a little further before I could open fire. He looked both ways, but I don't think he saw me. He seemed to be brandishing something in his hand. Then, as if willed by me, he stepped out of the doorway. It was then as he did this, he looked my way and saw me. He froze as he registered the gun I was aiming at him from about three metres away. I could have shot him straight away, but I waited instead. I'm not sure why I did this; maybe I was enjoying the moment, taking it all in.

The quietness resumed around us as we both stood there, statue-like, me holding the gun aimed towards his chest, finger exerting a small amount of pressure on the trigger, him, fearful looking, staring between the gun and my eyes, probably wondering who the hell I was and why I wanted to kill him. He might also have been calculating whether I had the bottle to shoot him.

I wondered why he'd been so rash and come out after me, knowing that I had a gun. Whatever made him take that decision, he'd be regretting it now. I saw that the object he was holding was a baseball bat. I could see in his eyes that he knew was powerless to do anything about the situation

I was tempted to strike up a conversation with him. I'd have loved to find out more about his life and how he'd managed to get himself into this situation whereby I was going to kill him. However, I knew that at any moment he would take a chance and lunge forward. If I wasn't quick enough, I'd lose my golden opportunity to complete the task. He didn't look as though he was going to try and talk me out of shooting him.

I wasn't sure if he moved forward as I pulled the trigger or whether it was a combination of my imagination and his body jerking as the bullet hit him. But if he did, I'd fired just in time. He didn't fall over straight away, he lunged forward as though he had a sharp pain in his stomach. It was as though, due to the physical size of him, it took longer to take effect. He was like a larger-than-life figure, nearing his end but refusing to give in easily. I moved a bit nearer to him and fired two more shots to his head to finish the job.

This was my cue to turn and sprint. I'd stayed around longer than I should have. I'd been doing a bit of exercise recently, gym work and running. This was the chance to put it to practical use.

I was on a buzz as I got home that night and I didn't sleep properly until the next afternoon. I played the moment over and over in my mind where I was standing facing him, ready to fire. In reality, it had probably been only a few seconds that we stood there like that. But in my mind, it had gone on for hours. I loved that moment, it was incredible, and if it was possible, I'd relive it.

I'd now killed my fourth target and I was beginning to feel like a true professional. I wasn't sure how lucky I'd been, but I felt psychologically I was dealing with it better. It mattered to me much less about the possibility of being caught. I felt a bit more secure as though I was becoming untouchable. Although, I realised this was dangerous and I knew the worst thing I could do was become complacent.

A few days after I'd killed Donovan, Kez phoned. She acted as though nothing had happened and that we'd only spoken yesterday. She certainly didn't mention the last phone conversation we'd had that had ended with each us annoyed at the other.

After a few pleasantries, she got to the point of the call and asked me to meet her on Sunday evening, in the pub we'd met at before. I was free and didn't decline the offer, even though, as I was accepting it, I knew I should be telling her that I wanted to end our weird little affair and that it was for the best if she didn't phone me again. I felt a pang of excitement once I'd put the phone down and our meeting had been arranged. It had been nearly three weeks since I'd spoken to her and would be six weeks since we'd last met up. It concerned me that, despite this, I still felt like a love-struck teenager. Perhaps foolishly, I was willing to forgive her for the lack of contact and her reaction when we'd last spoke.

Sunday arrived and I sat in the pub at the time of our arranged meeting, very much looking forward to seeing her. She failed to live up to her previous good punctual record and turned up twenty minutes late. I was beginning to think she wouldn't come at all. She walked over to where I was sitting and gave me a brief smile. She didn't apologise for being late, but I didn't expect her to. I was blown away by her looks once more. She was delectable. As usual, she hadn't even made much of an effort either. She had used very little make up and was casually dressed for the occasion in jeans and a hoody.

Once she had bought some drinks for us and sat down, we chatted away about nothing significant. We didn't even discuss what we'd been up to over the last six weeks. Our conversation was very natural and even though I wanted there to be, there was undoubtedly a connection between us. Although, there were so many things left unsaid. It was as though there was an unwritten rule about what we were and weren't allowed to talk about. Anything major occurring in our lives seemed to be avoided. Up until my change of life, I would have welcomed this type of conversation, but now I had things I wanted to talk about and share. Kez didn't allow me to do this initially as she seemed to control the conversation. However, after a couple of drinks and an hour or so, she suggested moving on somewhere else. I agreed but spontaneously said, "You're in control of this relationship."

"What do you mean?" she replied.

"Well, you dictate everything we do. I just seem to be your puppet and do whatever you want me to do."

She grinned but didn't say anything. A few minutes later we were heading back to her sister's flat, having stopped on the way for a takeaway.

We sat in the kitchen as we had the last time I'd been invited back. We drunk cans of beer whilst eating the takeaway food. I felt very relaxed all of a sudden and not in need of the joint that Kez rolled after we'd finished our curry. We sat in silence for what seemed like ages, quiet contemplation. Finally, Kez spoke and broke the silence.

"So, do you still think about your ex?" The question took me back and brought me out of my chilled mood.

"Sometimes, why do you ask?"

"How long did you go out together?"

"About six months." It had been six and a half but I didn't want to sound like it mattered.

"Not long then, but I can tell you were hurt."

"I'm not sure you know me that well," I replied, but inside I was annoyed she was right.

She grinned. I gave her the benefit of the doubt that this was more to do with the side effects of the joint than her taking the piss.

"Do you care about my feelings then?" I asked trying to deflect the conversation.

"Not really," she said in a very straight way that hurt me if I was truthful but was determined not to show. I grinned to keep up the facade.

"I'm not sure you're a very nice person," I said, "or are you asking about my ex because you're jealous?"

"Fuck off," she spontaneously replied and in a tone that suggested my question was ridiculous.

I was close to asking her why she kept seeing me, but I felt like I knew her well enough not to bother. I couldn't imagine for one minute I'd get a straight answer.

"It's OK to miss her, you know," she said in a caring tone, the irony of which was not lost on me given her previous words.

"I didn't say it wasn't, but it's not really any of your business what I think."

She laughed at this but didn't respond. The silence resumed for a while and then she started laughing again. The earlier conversation and paranoia instantly made me think she was laughing at me.

"What?" I said in a slightly irritated tone, still a bit riled with her previous comments.

"I don't know why, but I was thinking of a time I was with my friend and we were travelling on the tube. We were going somewhere; I can't even remember where now…" she giggled again, as obviously the tale was funny to her. "We only had enough money for one ticket and for some stupid reason thought that would be enough to get us through the ticket gates at the other end. My friend came up with this stupid idea that if there was a man guarding the gate when we reached the top of the escalator one of us should distract him, whilst the other one went through." She burst into fits of laugher again; I waited patiently for her to carry on with the story, but also starting to giggle myself now, her laughter becoming infectious. "Anyway, it was the worst idea. She said she'd fall over dramatically so he'd go over to help and then I'd slip through,' she continued, still through intermittent laughing. "So, I stood a couple of steps behind her and when she got to the top, she did the most stupid fake and overly dramatic fall I've ever seen. She was rolling around like a weedy footballer. But believe it or not, it worked. The guy on the gate came rushing over to her to see if she was all right and I stepped past and out of the station whilst he was checking on her. Whenever I think about that fall it always makes me laugh," and sure enough she started again. I was laughing harder now as well, still more at her laughing than the story. I had no idea why she was telling me it, particularly after the conversation we'd just had.

"Eventually she calmed herself down a bit and after a couple of attempts started talking again. Funny thing was, we were so stupid that I'd kept hold of the ticket instead of giving it to her, so once she'd picked herself up and declared she was all right the guy asked her for it and she realised that I'd got it. I've never seen her run so fast." This time my laughter was at the story rather than just Kez laughing. We both kept laughing until it hurt.

The next morning, I left the flat feeling groggy from the excesses of the night before but in good spirits. I didn't ponder on my relationship with Kez. For once, I would enjoy the moment.

Chapter Nine

Over the next few weeks, I concentrated my time on getting my licence to be a lorry driver. I saw Kez a couple of times during this period, always at her instigation. I gave up trying to contact her and instead waited for her to get in touch. It wasn't an ideal situation, but then I didn't want a proper relationship. Something casual suited me if I could reign my feelings in. It was quiet on the hitman front, with nothing in my P.O. Box on the occasions I checked.

My test came up again and fortunately I passed this time, being definitely more focused than on the previous occasion. Then it was time to start registering with agencies to find some work. I was looking forward to it, spending time on the road. It seemed like a job that I could do and switch off from everything else whilst being away. However, before I had a chance to do my first job, I was presented with an envelope at the post office. It didn't set my heart racing like it did before. I felt I was getting used to this work. I took it home as usual and opened it whilst making a cup of tea. What I was greeted with struck me out of my calm persona. It was the picture that I took in first. I didn't read the note that came with it. I started looking at it in disbelief. My heart sank. This changed everything. I was staring at a picture of my ex-girlfriend. Many questions raced around my head. Strangely, upon reflection, I was also trying to work out when the picture had been taken; it seemed a while back, possibly before I started seeing her. She was wearing some clothes I didn't recall her having. She was leaning against a gate and I couldn't recognise where it was. What was I going to do? How the hell had she got herself in to this situation? More to the point, how the hell had I got myself into this situation? I couldn't go through with it, could I? I had struggled to get over her, even Kez could tell that, annoyingly.

I didn't sleep much during the next few days, the task I had been given haunting me. There were so many thoughts going around my head I couldn't properly focus on anything. The only very small positive was that I hadn't been given a deadline to carry out the deed; this at least gave me time to think, which I was doing a lot of, without formulating any clear plan. My thoughts ranged from telling her that she was in danger (from me ironically), to trying to find out who my bosses were, to just carrying it out and moving on. None of them were ideal. I didn't go out during this time, as tempting as it was to go to the pub and drown my sorrows. Eventually, my isolation was broken by Kez contacting me. She had invited me to see a band she had tickets for. In true Kez style, she told me that she was supposed to go with someone else, but they'd cancelled on her and I was the only person she could think of to go with. I agreed, even though I knew I should tell her to stick it.

The event turned out to be good, the sort that begs the question why I didn't go to more things like it, as well as temporarily distracting me from my turmoil. We headed back to her sister's flat afterwards. Her sister was nearly always away so Kez was spending more time there. Kez had told me that her sister was going to rent it out soon. I think Kez was disappointed about this; it was a good retreat for her. God knows what Gaz thought she was up to whilst she was staying there, I wouldn't have trusted her if I'd been him.

Before I'd gone out, I'd been determined not to mention my dilemma, but I knew deep down I wouldn't need much encouragement and Kez was realistically the only person I could talk to. For all her failings, she was removed from the rest of my life. Sure enough, shortly after arriving back at that flat, she asked me about how my work was going and whether I'd had any jobs recently. I looked at her, wondering how to answer, and she instantly picked up something was not right.

"What's happened?" she enquired eagerly.

"Nothing, but I was given a job a few days back."

"Go on," she responded, seemingly keen to hear what I had to say.

"Well, it's unbelievable, I can't get my head round it, but it's a contract on my ex!"

"Your ex-girlfriend!" she exclaimed and I could instantly tell this pleased her. Her pleasure at my predicament instantly annoyed me.

"I knew I'd get sympathy from you," I snapped.

"Sorry, I know it's bad. I can't believe it." Her brief apology surprised me, as small as it was, it wasn't normal for her to do so.

"Nor can I."

"What are you going to do?"

"I don't know," I said holding my head in my hands. The few hours respite at being at the gig had now come to a harsh end and I was back to reality.

"You could tell them that you don't want to do it."

I looked at her puzzled. What was she talking about? Then I realised that, despite what I'd told her, she didn't understand properly how it worked.

"Well, I could do if I had a fucking clue who they were."

It was Kez's turn to look puzzled.

"What do you mean?"

I explained the situation again and how I had no way of contacting my employers. She listened to me, open mouthed, taking in my every word. I could tell that this was of great interest to her and it appeared as though this was the best entertainment she'd had for a while. At the end, she had that thoughtful face she has occasionally when she's thinking of her next words. It was one of her looks that I found the most attractive.

"You've really dug yourself into a hole, haven't you?" she said, offering no help at all. "In fact, you're a bit fucked, I'd say," she said showing a complete lack of sympathy to my predicament. Although this annoyed me, in reality I knew I didn't deserve any.

"Another problem is that even if I do decide to do it, I've got links to her. The others I'd not known beforehand. If I carry it out, the police are likely to look me up at some point, having been known to her for a while."

"So, what do you think will happen if you don't do it?" she asked.

"I don't know, but I suspect it wouldn't be good."

"And you don't know of any way to find them."

"As I've said, no. I've no idea who they are."

"You say you were given a number. Have you still got it?"

"Erm, I think so."

"You can probably trace that. In fact, I think I know someone who could help you if you want."

"Possibly, but like I said, I'm not sure I want to."

"Well then, you've got no choice, have you?" she said with a grin on her face. "Your beloved ex will have to go." At this point she got up and left the room, leaving me thinking two things. Did Kez care about anything, and that maybe her advice was right.

Killing her should be easy, compared to some of the tasks I'd had. After all, I knew her, was aware of her movements and when I was likely to find her on her own. She often went out with her friend on Mondays to an exercise class, followed by a couple of drinks in a nearby pub. I used to joke with her that the drinks negated the benefit of her earlier efforts. Her friend lived in a different direction, so they parted their ways after the pub. The way home for her was quiet and dark and I remember telling her to be careful.

I left Kez's the next morning. As usual, we'd made no definite plans about when we'd next meet.

The next couple of days, I went through phases of thinking I'd do it, to trying to think of ways out of it, like moving abroad or somehow confronting my boss or bosses. What I had decided to do was go and see her. The more I thought about, it the more intrigued I was as to how she had managed to get herself into this situation. She was quite straight and therefore I couldn't see why someone would want her dead. This more and more led me to think what I had been trying to avoid, that I was being tested and the people ordering me about were watching me and knew my life. It was too much of a coincidence that they had given me this job without knowing the connection. This I didn't like the thought of, as if it was the case, I was completely under their control.

Going to see her would be fraught with risk if I did go ahead with it. I'd be much more in the frame for killing her if I had only just seen her, compared to being an ex who'd had no contact for a while. However, I wanted to find out more, either that she was in trouble or there was nothing to it and I was being set up.

I went to her house the next weekend. I had no idea who she

lived with now. When I was going out with her, she lived with two friends, but for all I knew she could be living with her boyfriend now. I also couldn't think of a good excuse to see her other than for a catch up, which would make it awkward.

As I knocked on the door, I felt nervous. This was ridiculous, I thought. Why was I anxious about a conversation with her when I'd done much more high-risk things in the last few months? Her friend answered and looked intrigued to see me. We'd only met a couple of times. She left me standing at the door whilst she went to get her. I could hear a bit of talking before I was greeted by her. She did not look overly impressed to see me. I somehow managed to persuade her to let me in and she reluctantly made me a cup of tea. She asked me what I had come for. I told her that I just wanted to catch up. We'd not parted on bad terms and it was nice to keep in touch. She understandably looked suspicious and I could tell that she wanted to tell me to piss off. Fortunately, she was too nice to do this and I took advantage by asking her lots of questions about what she was up to. She humoured me by giving me information on her friends, family and her job. There was nothing untoward about any of it and she seemed her normal self. Although, there was a good chance if anything was wrong in her life, she wouldn't let me know. However, there seemed an air of calmness about her that belied any possibility something had gone majorly wrong in her life. We parted after about an hour, me asking her to keep in touch and her very half-heartedly saying she would.

I returned home, with a greater sense of paranoia about me. These people, whoever they were, knew a lot about me.

Over the next few days, my mind wondered back and forth on what I should do, but I eventually came to a decision. I needed to do this a bit differently though, to try to remove myself form the frame. When I was sixteen, I was out with one of my mates who was not exactly law abiding. We'd managed to get hold of some fags and a couple of cans of lager and before I knew it, he'd persuaded me we should steal a car and do some joy riding. He wasn't particularly clever at school, but he was an artist when it came to breaking into and hot wiring a car. Fortunately, I'd taken in what he'd done and managed to retain some of this information. It might come in handy over the next few days.

I wanted an old car, something the police wouldn't pay much attention to if reported missing. On the Sunday night in the early hours, I went out looking for it and found a perfect match on a dodgy estate. It was about fifteen years old and didn't look remotely loved. As long as it worked, it would be ideal. My old mates' trick worked, especially on a car this age, without the anti-theft mechanisms installed on newer models. I was in and away within a couple of minutes. I needed to find somewhere to hide it until Monday evening. I didn't want to put it anywhere connected to me. Asking any friends who had a garage was out of the question. Instead, I took it to a station car park a few miles away and left it there, having bought a ticket from the machine, so that it didn't get any unwanted attention the next day. I'd have to take the risk it wasn't found by the police in the meantime, the owner having likely reported the theft.

The next evening, I went back and fortunately it was still there. I picked it up and drove it to the hit point where I laid in wait. I guessed there was probably a half hour window of when she was likely to leave the pub. The road I was parked in was quiet with not too much lighting, so perfect. Sure enough, as I predicted, she appeared from a side alleyway that led into the road I was in. She would cross the road into a car park that was a cut through to her home. I had just enough time to double round to the car park entrance. As I entered, I could see her making her way through it towards where I'd now positioned the car. As I saw her, I accelerated. The car wasn't a Ferrari by any means, but it was small and therefore could reach forty quickly. I remembered seeing one of those government safety adverts, saying that at that speed a pedestrian has no chance. She stopped in her tracks as she saw the car speeding towards her, blinded partly by the lights. I could see her think for a split second—was the car headed for her? —and then the panic as she realised it was. At the last moment she tried to dive out the way, but it was too late. There was a loud thud as the car hit her and she flew up, clipping the front windscreen before disappearing over the back of the car. I broke sharply, stopped and turned around. I could see her lifeless on the floor. I didn't want to take any chances, though. I quickly turned off the lights to stop anybody who had heard the bang looking and trying to see the number plates. I then reversed back towards and straight over her. I didn't check on her after that. I drove out of there as quickly as I could, but trying not to drive too crazily to attract attention. After a minute or two, I turned the lights back on and carried on driving.

 I felt numb afterwards, not the usual buzz I'd felt with the others, but also not emotional about what I'd just done

 The car didn't have too much petrol in it, but I'd predicted this; the owner of a car like this would rarely fill it up more than required. I stopped after a while, by which point it was almost empty. I'd put two jerry cans of fuel in the boot earlier and I tipped these into the tank. I headed out of London and towards a lake I'd identified as a place I could get rid of the car. If I dumped the car anywhere, I'd be taking a risk forensically, given I would have almost certainly have left traces in the car. I was much more paranoid about this with my strong connection to the victim. I found a quiet area and stayed in the car a couple of hours before I pushed it in the lake. It wasn't a very nice journey back home, what with a lot of walking and eventually a very early train back into town. I had a lot of sleep to catch up on.

Two days after I got back home, I heard from Kez again. I think she found my life drama intriguing, leading to her wanting to see me more to catch up on the latest. We met in our usual pub, and the first thing she told me was she'd spoken to her friend who could find out the location of a phone number.

"How does he do that?" I asked.

"You should know better than to ask things like that," she retorted. She was right, although I was intrigued as to how it was done.

"OK, I'll give you it. It's at home somewhere. Although, I'm not sure what I'm going to do with the information once I have it. And anyway, the phone is probably in a vacant office somewhere, or monitored remotely."

"Maybe, but it's the only lead you have. Don't you want to find out who these people are?"

"Yes and no. I can hardly go to them and resign or ask for early retirement, can I?"

"Why not? You've done a fair bit of work for them from what I understand. Anyway, any more thoughts on what you're going to do about your latest job?"

I didn't want to tell her the deed was done. This one seemed a bit too much to trust her with. Instead, I just told her about my visit to her house and how I thought it couldn't be anything she was involved in.

"So, you're the common denominator. The mystery grows." Once again, I could tell she was enjoying all this.

"It would seem that way. If I do go ahead with this job, I

wonder what they will have next for me. There must be a reason why they've given me this one. After all, it's costing them a lot of money. I've already received an upfront payment. So, it can't just be for fun that they are doing this. There has to be some reason for it."

"So, all the other people have been completely random, as far as you are concerned. There is no connection to you, that you know of?"

"No, I've never met any of them before and most lived a long way away. I assumed that up until now, it's purely been contract killing. Someone wants somebody bumped off, goes into the black market and finds a firm who are willing to do it. Then the job gets assigned to me."

"Well, unless your ex has pissed someone off sufficiently for someone to take a contract out on her?"

"No," I responded. "She's too nice, too straight. Now if it was you, I could believe it." I laughed. I couldn't resist the dig, but what I said was true.

"Yep, you're probably right," she replied, seemingly taking it as a compliment.

After we'd finished at the pub, we went our separate ways. She hadn't invited me back to her sister's place, which I didn't know how to take. She'd made some excuse about having to be somewhere early the next day, but I wasn't convinced. I still didn't have a clue where the relationship was going. One thing I did think of, though, was if I did continue seeing her, I would either have to carry on my lie about not killing my ex or come clean. That was a problem for another day. I did contact her the next day just to give her the phone number.

After what had seemed like a hectic period, I took the chance to relax a bit. I stayed at home during the days watching television and went down the Crooked Billet regularly to catch up with my mates, something I hadn't done so much of recently. Then I got my first booking as a lorry driver, which was a few days' job going up to Scotland. I enjoyed this and the sinister parts of my life were forgotten about. When I got back there was nothing in my P.O. Box, nor a message from Kez, which I had half suspected. It been a few weeks since I last saw her and I wondered if she'd decided it was over. I certainly wasn't going to contact her. But just when I'd convinced myself it was, I returned home one night having been out with my mates to find a message from her asking me to call her. She said she had some information on the phone number from her friend. I'd forgotten about it, but wasn't going to pass the opportunity to find out more. After all, I didn't have to do anything with the information. I went to bed, thinking I'd call her the next day. I was woken the next morning by the phone. I answered after a few rings, tired and on the edge of being hungover. It was Kez.

"You're keen," I said once I realised it was her.

"Didn't you get my message?" She sounded a little exasperated. It was typical her. She hadn't liked it that I hadn't got in touch as soon as she'd called.

"Yes, I got back late last night." I could hear a small sigh, as if she couldn't believe I had the audacity to go out the night she wanted to speak to me.

"So, what did you find out?" I asked, remembering why she'd called.

"Let's meet later and I'll tell you." I was certain this was done just for her to wrestle back control. She was going to tell me when she wanted to, not when I asked.

We arranged to meet at our usual place. Part of me wanted to tell her to not bother, given that she'd acted like a petulant child, but I wanted to find out what she knew.

"She was late, but came over with a drink and, as always, looked stunning. I knew better than to ask her straight away what I wanted to know. I was pretty sure I'd have to wait until she was ready. She was talkative, though, and told me she'd had a busy couple of weeks and had also been away. I asked her how Gaz was."

"That's finished," she replied.

"Has it?" I responded, not being able to hide my surprise.

"I thought you might be pleased," she smiled. Although, I wasn't certain how she'd deduced that. It was probably her ego making this assumption. I didn't know what to think about it.

"So, what happened?"

"Oh, he was just being an idiot so I told him what he could do. I'd had enough of him."

"But I thought that he was financially good for you," I laughed.

"All good things and that..." she replied, also laughing. "Anyway, I have my ways of getting cash," she said in a way that I knew meant that she wouldn't tell what they were even if I asked.

"So, you've been patient in waiting for the information I have," she said with a teasing smile. Looking at her, I hated and loved her at the same time.

"What did you find out?" I said as casually as I could, not wanting to sound over keen. She paused, maintaining her smile for dramatic effect.

"Well, that number is linked to a house lived in by an old lady."

"Really," I replied, genuinely surprised. "Where?"

"Oh, somewhere up North, in the back of beyond."

"What else do you know?" I asked, sensing by looking at her that there was more.

"Well, when we learnt where the number was, we thought it was worth a look to see what goes on there."

"You went there?" I asked, not hiding the disbelief in my voice. Why would she go there when she wasn't directly involved in all of this?

"Yes! How else were we going to find out what is going on? You should be pleased, I'm trying to help you out," she said admonishingly.

I was completely thrown by this news, caught between being flattered that she'd gone to such lengths to help me and suspicions as to what her true motives were for the effort she had made.

"So, what did you find out?"

"Well, as I said, we discovered there was an old lady living at this house. It's like an old cottage."

"We?" I asked." This was immediately met with a look that said, "I'm not going to answer that."

"Go on," I said knowing better than to pursue my previous question. In some ways it was best I didn't know.

"So, after a while of watching the place, two burly blokes turned up and went in. They could have been relatives, but looked distinctly out of place. I've got pictures of them."

She pulled some photos from her bag. I was bemused at the levels she'd gone to. She and her accomplice had done a full reconnaissance job.

"Do you recognise them?" She asked.

I studied the photos for a few seconds, half expecting to see H. He wasn't in the photo and I racked my brains to see if I could recognise either of the two large-looking blokes in the photo.

"No, don't think I've seen either of them before."

Kez looked disappointed. "It's likely they've got something to do with all this."

"So, tell me more. When did they go in there and how long for?"

"See, you're pleased I made the effort now, aren't you?" I didn't respond, just rolled my eyes instead. "We saw them go in there a couple of times, maybe for about an hour on both occasions."

This was all well and good, I thought, but it hadn't got me any further in solving the mystery of who was behind this. I didn't want to appear ungrateful to Kez, even if I did find it strange that she had gone to the lengths she had. Her actions were almost as much as a puzzle as to who was behind it.

"Well, I appreciate your help, but I guess me not recognising them means we haven't got much further." I said, trying to show gratitude for her efforts. "Can I get you a drink?"

"Hang on, I haven't finished yet." Kez said with a hint of annoyance.

"What do you mean?" I asked.

"Well, it would have been stupid to leave it at that, given the effort and information we'd got so far."

"I guess so. Do you have more?" I asked.

"Well, obviously the two guys didn't live there, so once we'd seen them go in a couple of times, we decided to concentrate our efforts on them. See if we could find out more about them." She paused for effect, seeing that she had my full attention again. I waited patiently for her to continue.

"So, after the second time they left the house, we followed them."

"Where did they go? Did they live local?"

"We lost them shortly after following them in the car."

"Oh," I said, not hiding my disappointment well.

"But we got the number plate of the car," she continued, once she'd let me think again her story was over. I could tell she was enjoying this a lot.

"The car's registered to an address in London, not too far from here. Of course, it could have been stolen, but sure enough one of the guys turned up there a couple of days later."

Now I was impressed. I couldn't believe how much she had ascertained and clearly her accomplice had access to information they probably shouldn't have. I wasn't going to give Kez the pleasure of asking this, knowing the negative response I'd receive.

"Christ, you have been busy," I said.

"I can give you the address, but first I think you need to make a contribution to my friend's work," she said, raising her eyes.

I was slightly affronted given that I hadn't requested any of this information, but then what they'd found out could prove very useful.

"OK, let me know how much," I responded.

She looked at me and I could tell she was weighing up what to say, perhaps wondering what she could get away with.

"I reckon five hundred should cover it."

I held in a gasp. I wasn't expecting that much. A small smile formed on her face, whilst I was deciding how to respond. She had a habit of putting on certain looks that changed my mood instantly. I knew she was doing it, but I still fell for it. I could afford it, so it wasn't an issue.

"It's all for your friend, is it?"

Her face broke into a broader smile and she said in barely more than a whisper, "Of course."

"OK, let me know when to give you the money."

"Have you got it at your place?"

"Ermm, I may do," I said, knowing full well that I did. I still hadn't solved my little issue of where to put the cash that I had come into.

"Well, let's head back there then after these," Kez said, nodding towards the drinks on the table. As it turned out, that was the last time we slept together. Why this was I'm not sure, but it was the start of a gradual decline in our already rocky relationship.

Chapter Ten

The next morning, after Kez had left, I sat looking at the address. She was right, it was close to where I lived. I wondered what to do. I wasn't quite at the stage where I was desperate to get out, but the last assignment with my ex-girlfriend had shaken me. It was unnecessary and I was very much starting to resent the hold these people had on me. Added to the fact that all along I'd had the nagging thought in the back of my head of what happens when I've had enough? If I could find them, I could only think of two options to extricate myself from what I'd committed to: either speak to them and negotiate my way out of whatever I was involved with, or make them my next contract. The first seemed a tall order. I doubted these people would be willing to compromise and would want everything on their terms. As for the second option, this could work and was slightly appealing, but despite Kez and her accomplice's handiwork, I still didn't know how many of them there were or how the whole operation was run. I could start doing a little surveillance on the address and try to find out more. I'd have to be careful, though, as they knew me, and I certainly didn't want them to catch me snooping around.

With this on my mind, the next day, I went to check my box at the post office and, sure enough, there was an envelope there. This was typical timing and my first thought, before even opening it, was what my plan of action was. Should I focus on finding them or carry out this job first? I was going to have to make my mind up quickly as there was a time limit on this job. It was a month, which was a reasonable amount of time, but whatever path I took I'd have to start surveillance soon.

Sitting back at home, looking at the details of my new assignment I was a little intrigued. Peter Shellard was fifty-one years old and of smart appearance. He lived in an affluent area and, although the people I'd been assigned so far were of varying backgrounds, he was nothing like any of them. I thought I'd check him out first before making a decision. The money for his life was more than double than anything I'd been paid before, which was enticing me in the direction of being a good employee. Additionally, they'd given me a disproportionally small upfront payment, so it wasn't financially tempting to pocket that and seek my way out of this.

The next day, I ventured out to the Home Counties where he lived. I'd set off early, aware that he may be off to work at the crack of dawn. I was right. Shortly after I was in position, he appeared from his substantial property. It had a nice drive enclosed by a large gate, with two new German cars parked in it. With property prices on the rise, it would have been worth a pretty penny. I followed him on foot, hanging back to try not to get noticed. As I suspected, he went to the local station, where I assumed he caught the train into the city. In that short period of time, I'd made up my mind. I was going to do it. Although, I hadn't got a good look at him, there was an element of arrogance there. It came across in the picture too. He had an aura of superiority that I didn't like, the type of guy that wouldn't give people from my background the time of day. This, coupled with his very middle-class house, made me decide the World would be a better place without him.

Given that it was likely he commuted to the city, getting an opportunity in the week would be difficult unless I could push him under a tube. I decided to see what Peter did at the weekend and see if a better opportunity lay there.

I returned Saturday morning and parked across the road. One of the cars had already gone from the driveway. I sat in my car, reading a magazine, hoping the people in the road were too busy enjoying their wealth to notice a working-class lad like me hanging around. About an hour later, a woman emerged from the house and drove off in the other car. Not long after that, a younger woman appeared and drove a smaller, cheaper, but still new car out of the garage. She was good looking and of classy appearance, obviously benefiting from Daddy's money.

I was getting bored and wondered what Peter was up to. I was tempted to drive off and come back the next day, but I didn't want the morning to be wasted so I hung on. My patience was rewarded as around lunch time he returned. He got out of the car and fetched a set of golf clubs from the boot. I wondered if this was a weekly hobby. Although time wasn't on my side, I decided to wait until the next week to find out.

I got there earlier the next Saturday and followed him in my car. There was little traffic, so it was easy to keep track of where he was going without being right behind him all the time. Sure enough, after about a twenty-minute drive he pulled into a golf club. I followed him in but parked the other side of the car park. I could still see him, and he got out and made his way into the club house with his golf bag. I sat there and thought of how I could do this. The golf club was cut out from a forest. The surrounding trees providing plenty of cover. I needed a rifle. Easy to say, but difficult to obtain; this wasn't the US. I thought about the different ways of coming about one. I could go back to Jason or via Kez, but I'd prefer not to go back to the same source. I could also try to steal one, but that in itself wouldn't be easy; I'd have to either find a gun shop, and they wouldn't be easy to penetrate, or find a person who had one. Even then, I knew there was a requirement to keep them locked away. Ironically, I imagined Peter having one, but I wasn't going to try that. I'd need to find another way.

In the meantime, I studied a map of around the golf club. There was plenty of opportunity to get in over a fence and hide in the trees, lying in wait.

That week, Kez phoned me. We went for a curry together; the primary motive of her wanting to meet up seemed to be to find out if I'd done anything about following up on her lead with the address she had given to me. As always, I ended up telling her more than I'd intended to. She was interested to hear about my new assignment, but seemed disappointed I'd put off any thoughts about following up on the information she'd provided me.

"You know they're using you. Can't you see how much risk you are taking?"

"Of course they are using me. But they do pay me well. You should see how much I'm getting for this job," I replied. "And as for being risky, I'm not stupid, of course I'm taking risks. I've been doing that since it started."

"Yes, but aren't you worried the police are getting closer to finding you?"

"I try not to think about that. So far, so good though. They haven't darkened my door yet," I said, touching the wooden table we were sat at superstitiously, despite not believing in that sort of thing.

"You don't know what I mean do you?" She looked at me with an air of disbelief.

"No, what do you mean?" I asked, suddenly concerned. She had a habit of making me look stupid and I feared what was coming. But she delayed what she must have been about to tell me with another question.

"Don't you watch the news?"

"No, I find it depressing," I replied flippantly, wanting her to get to the point.

"Well, it seems as though they've found a link, with your murders," she spoke softly so nobody around could hear. Not that there were many people in the restaurant and the waiters certainly didn't look interested in what we had to say.

"What, how do you know these are my murders?"

She gave me a look of contempt. Another habit of hers, once my stupidity had been drawn out.

"Well, the coincidence is quite high. Random murders over the country. Nobody caught yet. Shootings, mainly. I don't confess to being brain of Britain, but from what you've told me, who else can it be? Also…" An accusatory look came over her face. "… why didn't you tell me you'd done your ex in after all?" She said this louder than she meant to, which made me flinch. She apologised instantly and looked around. Still, no one looked interested in what we were talking about. She then relayed her sentence more quietly. "You've got a real nasty streak. I wouldn't have said you had it in you. I've met some dodgy people, but not many who would do that!"

I was a bit dumbstruck. Because I'd hidden myself from the news, it hadn't seemed as real. I'd caught the odd news headline on a paper or billboard, but I'd blanked it out. If I ever picked up a paper, I only read the sports section. But Kez telling me now made me realise that my actions would be known all over the country.

"So, you said something about a connection?" I replied, as this was what I wanted to find out more about, but also because I didn't want to talk about my ex.

"Yes, the police made a statement that they've connected three or maybe four, I can't remember exactly, of the murders. I don't think your ex was one of them though. They might be closing in on you."

"Yes, but other than the obvious, I had no history with any of them beforehand. So, whilst there is no link to my ex, there's no real concern." I said this more for my benefit rather than hers.

"True, but maybe they've found traces of you."

"You're full of good news tonight," I responded.

"Well, I'm just trying to warn you. It may be time to quit."

"I think I will after this one."

"It might be one too many, why take the risk?"

"Because he's a tosser and worth quite a bit of cash."

Kez laughed at this. "I don't know whether your incredibly naive or just don't give a shit."

"Also, I don't have much time. If I don't carry out the job quickly, I'll miss my deadline and then these guys, whoever they are, may come after me. If I'm to go to them to try to stop all this, I want a bit of time to use the information you gave me to find out about them first."

Kez looked pensive for a few seconds and then said, "I see your point, but you are pushing your luck. Don't think I'm going to visit you in prison. I hate those places." I was slightly annoyed by the assumption I'd want her to visit if I did end up locked up for my crimes.

"So, do you know when you're going to do this one?"

"Hopefully soon, but I could really do with a rifle'" I said, realising again I'd said too much. I think Kez was a good outlet to speak to about all this; after all, I wasn't going to tell anybody else. As much as I liked to think I was independent, it was good to have a sound board. This was another attraction to Kez, which helped me put up with all her faults. I realised she was now laughing, having initially smiled at my previous sentence.

"You are unreal. Although I think I can help you there."

"What, you can get one?" I said in surprise, remembering how initially she didn't want to help with the silencer.

"Yeah, I think so."

"Through Gaz or Jason?"

"No, I told you. I'm not in touch with them anymore."

"You are very resourceful," I said, smiling and pleased that my problems might be solved.

"Hold your horses, I didn't say I can definitely help."

"Well, when can you find out? As I said, time is of the essence," I replied, knowing that Kez wasn't a girl who took kindly to being pushed into things and therefore might not like me hurrying her up.

"I'll be able to find out for you in the next couple of days."

"I could also do with an overview of how to use it," I said.

"Christ, you don't want much, do you? Sometimes I cannot believe you've managed to do what you've done. You come across as so amateurish."

"Thanks," I said sarcastically at the insult.

"Well, it's true. Either you are very lucky or somebody's looking out for you. As I said right from the start, you don't seem cut out for this game."

I laughed at this instead of arguing the point. It wasn't worth debating. She could think what she liked. We left the curry place and went our separate ways, Kez agreeing to be in touch soon about the rifle.

I waited nervously the next couple of days. I didn't like the situation and was conscious of the time passing. I was completely relying on her pulling though. I wasn't used to this. I'd worked on my own until now. I thought about a backup plan if Kez let me down and was struggling to come up with a good one. Fortunately, Kez phoned me with news that she could help. She wanted me to meet her and once again I found myself waiting for her at what had become our usual table at the pub we regularly met at. Despite her good news, I was still a bit on tenterhooks. Time was not on my side; the deadline was fast approaching. Kez waltzed in fifteen minutes late and talked about nothing in particular for the first half hour. I couldn't wait any longer.

"So, you can get one then?" I asked when there was a small pause in conversation.

She smiled. "Anyone would think you were using me. I worry you don't care about me and just want me for my services," she said sarcastically.

I rolled my eyes but didn't humour her with a response.

"Yes, but it's going to take a couple of weeks. They're out of stock at the moment."

This was exactly what I didn't want to hear. I had less than ten days going by the deadline. She saw the concern on my face. "What's wrong?" she asked. I was sure I'd told her about the deadline.

"I don't have that long. Can they not get it earlier?"

"It's not like ordering a book, you know," she retorted.

I sighed and said, "I guess it will have to do."

"Yes, it will," she chirped quickly. "No need to thank me."

"Sorry, I just don't have much time, that's all."

"Also, they will meet you to give you a quick brief on it, but it will be quick," she said with an emphasis on the quick. "I've had to do a lot of vouching for you, you're lucky to get anything at all."

I thanked her again and offered her a drink. At the bar, I thought about my predicament. In all likelihood I was going to do this job at least a couple of weeks after the deadline. I wondered how they'd react. I didn't like the situation, but it would be interesting to see what they did and whether it brought them out of the woodwork. Kez and I didn't discuss the subject after that. As we parted, she promised me she'd call as soon as it was ready. I had a nervous couple of weeks ahead of me.

Therefore, I played the waiting game, as I had nothing else to do. There was no point in chasing Kez every five minutes. She had told me, emphatically, that it will take as long as it takes. As for my employers, there was nothing I could do there either. It crossed my mind to find another way to do the job—after all, I'd done so before—but my plan was perfect. I just needed the tool to carry it out. I found it boring waiting and I didn't like not being in control. I couldn't even do any lorry driving as I didn't want to be away for a period of time that might mean missing Kez's call.

The deadline came and went. Three days later, Kez called. It was ready. Once again, she had pulled through for me. The cost was a lot more than I'd bargained for, but I was in no position to negotiate. A meeting was set up. I was to pick up Kez and then we'd drive there together. Parked outside her sister's flat, I waited for her to come out, nervously tapping the steering wheel. I'd have preferred not to have to meet the seller, but I knew I needed the instruction of how to use it. After a few minutes, the passenger door opened and Kez jumped in. She seemed to have plenty of energy about her, as though she was looking forward to this; the opposite of me.

"Thanks a lot, Kez, I appreciate this," I said, although asking myself why she was enjoying this. Maybe I wasn't one to talk, but I was concerned about her state of mind.

She chatted about nothing in particular during the twenty-minute drive to our destination. Although, I wasn't really listening to her. In between, she directed me as I drove and we pulled up outside a shabby-looking workshop situated underneath a railway viaduct. An old sign advertised car body repairs. Kez sensed my unease, in line with her tendency to read my moods. "You're nervous, aren't you?" she said as we got out of the car.

I thought briefly about denying it but realised there was no point. "Just a little," I retorted, forcing a smile. Not surprisingly, this seemed to amuse her.

We walked into the workshop past some beaten-up looking cars, one with a young lad, possibly an apprentice, working on the bodywork. One or two didn't look like they were worth the effort to get roadworthy. At the back, in the corner of the workshop, was a small office. We walked in to see a man sitting behind a desk on the phone. He looked up in mid-conversation and gave me the briefest of glimpses before moving his eyes towards Kez. He winked at her and pointed at the phone, mouthing that he wouldn't be long.

"Look, mate, I told you how it would look…"

"I don't care what the insurance company are saying." He was raising his voice and I wondered whether this was for our benefit. He was probably in his early fifties, unshaven, and wore wide, round rimmed glasses. His hair was starting to recede in a v either side of his forehead, the remaining hair cut short. On initial sighting, he had an appearance of a normal working-class guy. I could have been swayed by what I knew we were about to exchange, but his manner on the phone and the expressions he pulled gave an impression he was not to be messed with.

"I haven't got time for this, Jim, and you're beginning to annoy me. I suggest you leave it." With that, he firmly replaced the phone receiver in its holder and looked up.

"Kez, darling, good to see you."

"And you, Dave. How's it going?"

"Well, it would be better if I didn't have tossers annoying me all day," he said, nodding towards the phone.

"There's plenty about," Kez replied. I was starting to feel a bit of a spare part in the room as they continued their small talk. Apart from the initial glance, Dave hadn't acknowledged me at all. I wondered what it was with these people who did dodgy dealings. Obviously, they weren't pleasant people, but they liked to treat their customers with contempt.

After a couple of minutes, he stood and said, "Right, better get down to business." He walked to the door, brushing past me and still not making any effort to acknowledge me. "Follow me," he said as he walked across the workshop. He signalled to the young guy who appeared to be buffering up the bodywork of the car he was working on with an electrical tool. The lad switched it off and looked up. "Go and get us a cup of tea from the van will ya, Tom." The lad put down the tool and shuffled out towards the road reluctantly.

Dave tutted and mumbled something under his breath, seemingly unhappy with Tom's attitude. Once Tom was out of sight on his errand, Dave opened the boot of an old Vauxhall that looked like it had been rotting away at the back of the workshop. He lifted up a cover and then pulled out something long, that I assumed to be my purchase, wrapped in some sheets. Hardly an innovative hiding place, I thought, and I wondered what sort of quality the weapon would be given how small fry Dave seemed to be. He walked back to the office, the wrapped gun in his hands, beckoning us once more to follow him. It crossed my mind to ask why he made us walk over to the car when we were going back to his office, but I realised that antagonising him wouldn't be a good idea. Once back in his office, he motioned Kez to shut the door.

"Right, I was told you need some teaching in how to use one of these," he said, looking at me for once. The contempt was clear in his voice.

"Would be good," I replied.

"First things first, though." He looked at me again and momentarily I was confused as to what he meant and then the penny dropped. I pulled out an envelope from my inside jacket pocket that had a considerable amount of cash in it, more than I wanted to pay especially given how this was panning out. I was doubting the gun would work or that Dave would give me a good overview of its workings. He brightened up once confronted with lots of cash and became more talkative. We spent the next ten minutes going through the basics and I was pleased to discover that it wasn't going to be that difficult to handle. Kez and I departed the office with the weapon and a reasonable number of cartridges for it. As we did, Tom returned with Dave's tea. He glanced at the package, once again wrapped up in the sheets, and gave a confused look, clearly wondering what it was. We heard Dave reprimanding him for taking so long. This was ironic given his timing had been perfect, returning as soon as we'd finished. I felt sorry for him having to work there, even if my opinion of Dave had improved a little compared to when we first arrived. As in the style of Dave, I put the gun in the boot, hiding it away as best as I could, and Kez and I got in the car. She'd hardly spoken since the gun was handed over other than to say goodbye to Dave. I wondered how she knew him.

"He's all right Dave, isn't he?" I said to her as I drove away.

"Yep, certainly got you out of a hole."

"Is he a relative or something?" I said as casually as I could, hoping she would tell me the connection in the course of the conversation.

She laughed and said, "It's none of your business. Just be thankful I know him at all."

"I am," I sighed, once again disappointed that I'd still not found out anything about Kez. "I'm grateful to him for getting me the gun, even if I think I've paid well over the odds for it."

"You pay what you have to, it's not like you can get one on the high street. Anyway, you can afford it."

I said nothing in response, but I didn't like the way it was said. It made me think that was exactly what she'd told Dave and consequently the price had been hiked.

I dropped Kez off and made my way home, thinking about where I was going to hide the rifle. Kez's warning about the police making links between the murders had made me more nervous. If they came and searched my place and found a small armoury, I'd be in serious trouble. With this and my strange relationship with Kez on my mind, I entered my home. There was some post on the door mat, most of which looked like junk mail apart from one envelope that caught my eye. It was blank and didn't have a stamp or mark on the envelope. I left the rest there and picked up this one, putting the rifle down that I had carried in from the car. Inside was one sheet of paper with typed writing on it. I knew immediately what it was and wasn't surprised to receive it. The message was

"THE DEADLINE HAS EXPIRED. CARRY OUT THE

JOB IMMEDIATELY OR FACE THE CONSEQUENCES"

I looked at the rifle leaning up against the wall and was thankful I had it. Whatever the consequences were, they were not likely to be good, and I needed to act. Despite this, I did think that for now it was probably an idle threat to hurry me up. If they did something to me, then they would then need to find someone else to do their dirty work. Although, I didn't want to test this theory. The weekend was only a couple of days away and therefore I could carry out the job soon. It made me realise that it was time to get out. I didn't like the way I was being treated.

I passed the next couple of days in a state of paranoia. I didn't know how long "immediately" was and therefore spent a lot of time looking over my shoulder wherever I went. I slept, or tried to, with the gun under my pillow. I was grateful when the early hours of Saturday morning arrived, and I could take action. I felt prepared for the job. I'd done more research on the golf course during the period I was waiting for the rifle and felt confident. I drove to a car park used mainly by daytime walkers about a mile from the golf club. From there I would walk to the course and jump over a fence that bordered it. This was probably the most dangerous part in terms of being seen. I'd carried the gun in a sports bag. However, at three in the morning the roads would be quiet, and I was lucky in that this night was no different. Once inside the course, I made my way to a woodland area bordering one of the holes. The trees there were thick providing good shelter. Now was the boring part. Lying in wait. On the few occasions I'd observed him, Peter normally got to the club about seven. I was a few holes around the course, so I estimated he'd be within sight by about eight. I should be feeling exhausted given my lack of sleep over the last few days, but adrenaline was keeping tiredness at bay. I spent my time thinking about my predicament and what my actions would be, assuming everything went to plan that morning. I also thought about Kez. Despite her linking me up with Dave for the rifle, I'd had enough of her and thought about ignoring her the next time she called. I felt like our weird relationship had run its course, even if I would be severing ties with someone who clearly had some very handy contacts. Time went surprisingly fast and before I knew it the sun was up and the first golfers were making their way around. This provided plenty of sight practice, although I had to be careful on the odd occasion a wayward ball landed close to my vicinity. The spot I was in meant I could see the golfers through the trees as they reached the tee ahead, especially with the aid of a small pair of binoculars I'd brought with me. Then once they moved down the hole, they would be closer and in good range.

Sure enough, a little after eight o'clock, Peter and his two playing partners appeared up ahead on the tee. I watched them tee off and then start to walk in my direction. I was slightly concerned that Peter would hit his ball towards the other side of the fairway from me. I'd calculated that wherever he ended up I would have a shot, but it would be much closer and easier if he stayed in the fairway or to my side of it. Fortunately for me, he'd played a good shot and was positioned in the centre of the fairway. I settled into position, testing the sight to where he would be standing in a few moments. I suddenly felt very calm and the atmosphere around was serene. I was ready. The thought occurred to me that if I did escape this game after this hit, I would miss it in a way. The adrenaline rush and feeling after I carried out an assassination was like no other I'd experienced. He came into my sight, totally unaware what was about to happen. He positioned his golf trolley to the side of the ball and looked ahead to where the green was. He must have been thinking about what club to use. He eventually selected one and pulled it from his bag. He stood swinging for a while, practicing and probably picturing in his mind the shot he was going to play. Finally, he settled into position to play the shot. This was the moment. I had perfect sight of him. I had two shots, but I wanted to do it with one. Time seemed to move in slow motion as I pulled the trigger, having lined him up for the final time in the sight. The noise was close to deafening and there was recoil from the gun that Dave had warned me about. However, by the time this had an impact on the soft part of my shoulder, the cartridge was hurtling towards Peter. He collapsed in a heap. The shot was right on target. Part of me wanted to stay around to see the panic, confusion and horror of his two friends unfold, but of course I didn't have time. By the time they'd have taken in what had happened, I was fast making my way away from the scene. I had a plan to hide the sports bag with the gun in it in the woodland, a safe distance away from the shooting, so I wouldn't be seen running away with it. There was a risk it would be found, but I'd wiped it clean and would have to take the chance. I found the fence after this and jumped over. There was much traffic on the road it led onto, so I hoped nobody would take much notice of me. From there, I made my way back to my car.

Chapter Eleven

Even though I'd had very little sleep during the last few days, I was buzzing and full of energy, the latest hit putting me on a high. I went to the Crooked Billet that night and met up with a few mates I hadn't seen for a couple of weeks. Life had been a bit intense one way or another recently and it was good to have a few drinks and relax. Given my recent lack of practice on top of little sleep, it didn't take many drinks for me to start feeling it. I returned home later feeling satisfied with life. The next day I spent mostly in bed, hiding from a hangover and resting my tired body. I had additional good news on Monday, finding out I had some lorry driving work starting early on Tuesday, meaning I'd be away for a few days. This was perfect for me. I could get away and forget about recent events. I had one job to do first, though. I got up earlier on Tuesday morning than I needed to, making my way back to the golf course under the cover of darkness. I'd hidden the gun well and there was no sign that it had been disturbed.

I decided, whilst I was away, that I'd start my surveillance of the address Kez had provided me when I got back, and try to find out more about the people who were likely behind my killing spree. When I returned, I discovered Kez had left a message on my answer machine during my absence. I decided to ignore it.

The day after I got back from my driving job, I went to check my P.O. Box. I was expecting the second payment to be there. Annoyingly, it wasn't. Up until now, my employees had been very quick to send me the cash that I had been promised. This was one thing I couldn't fault them with. Although, the lack of final payment for this job had me concerned. Were they punishing me for not carrying it out within the specified time? That would seem harsh, not that I could do much about it. It would seem more reasonable if they reduced the payment. Although this wasn't a business of reason. Of course, the payment might still be on its way, but I had my doubts. All this did was make me want to find out more about them and a way to extricate myself from their illegal doings.

Over the next couple of days, I watched their house and tried to follow the two men Kez had showed me the photos of whenever I could. I didn't learn much. They didn't go out much together and there was no pattern to their comings and goings. They clearly didn't have any routine or normal jobs. Occasionally, I'd follow them to a pub where they may have met people, but I didn't go inside, concerned they'd spot me. The only thing that was mildly interesting was they had a couple of visits from the same guy. This was nothing major in itself, but he looked familiar and I racked my brains to remember where it might be from. However, even going over the last few months and the people I'd met during this time, as well as those I'd met through Kez, I couldn't place where I'd seen him before. So, other than this, I'd learnt nothing, and I was at a bit of a loss as to what to do. My three options remained: approach them and try to resolve the situation, take them out myself, or do nothing. None of them were perfect. My preferred one was eliminating them, but this had a few flaws. I couldn't be sure they were involved; I had no evidence to back it up, and I could be even less sure that there wasn't more of them, especially when I thought I was introduced to the whole thing by H. He certainly hadn't made an appearance during my surveillance.

I did decide to do some asking after him in the Crooked Billet, but this drew no results either. Nobody could remember seeing him for a long time. I thought about phoning Kez. She had a knack of helping me out when I was in a dilemma, but my pride prevented it. I'd been impressed with my self-restraint so far, resisting the urge to call her back. As the days drifted by, I realised that my only option was to confront them. Where and how I went about this was eluding me. I'd checked my box at the post office on a regular basis recently and it had been empty. I was more and more annoyed that they'd done me out of my second payment for Peter. However, on the positive side, I hadn't been given another job and I was wondering if this meant that they had stopped using me. After all, they could hardly give me another job until they paid me for the last one. I didn't care who they were, I wouldn't do another hit whilst I was still owed money.

A few days later, sitting at home watching some rubbish on daytime, there was a knock at the door. I didn't give much thought whilst walking to answer it as to who it may be, unaware of the shock I was about to receive. Two men in suits stood at the door. Before I'd had time to think, they had introduced themselves, names that I didn't register, and were showing me police identification. They seemed to be edging into my home before I'd even granted permission. I knew I didn't have a choice. I had to comply and remain as calm as I could. I offered them a cup of tea, hoping they'd say yes, so I could collect my thoughts in the kitchen whilst I made it. But either they were wise to this or weren't thirsty, as they were sitting down on my sofa barely seconds after I received a negative to my offer and were dispensing with any pleasantries by launching into what this was about. I braced myself for the worst and struggled to make sense of the words they were saying, yet as they sat there waiting for my response, I realised that they had asked me about my ex-girlfriend. Of the six murders that I'd carried out, this was the one that I thought about the least. I'd pushed it to the back of my head, blanked it out as much as possible. Of the others, particularly the last, I looked back on with a bit of pride, but not this one. I hadn't liked the way I'd gone about it.

"Yes, I heard what happened to her, it was terrible. Do you know who did it?'

"We wouldn't be here if we knew the answer to that," came a blunt response from the older one, whose manner I found irritating; that added to his condescending tone. He had flared nostrils and dark, beady eyes. He was also overweight; a bad diet was my guess. Surely, though, they weren't playing the good cop, bad cop routine you see on television.

"So, when did you last see her?" the other one asked. I knew I couldn't lie. They'd probably talked to her friend who she lived with and already knew the answer.

"I'm not sure exactly, but I think it wasn't long before it happened," I said as casually as I could.

"But at this point the relationship was over between you?" Once again, a more aggressive tone from "bad cop".

"Yeah, it had been over for quite a while," I said as though it was obvious.

"So why did you go and see her then?"

"I thought I'd catch up with her, see how she was. It wasn't like we broke up on bad terms." I wondered how much they knew and if they had anything on me. They could have, but despite my initial surprise at their visit, I was always likely to come up in their enquiries at some point. Given they hadn't arrested me yet,

I was hopeful it was the latter.

"How did you break up?"

"Good question," I said. The older one sighed at this. It was if he didn't have the time to waste on me and wanted to get through their questions as soon as he could. I took this as a good sign.

"We, I mean she, decided it wasn't working." I said.

"Were you unhappy about that?" the younger one said pouncing on my correction. Now I looked at him with more scrutiny, he was very young, especially to be out of uniform. He had a more pleasant look about him, though, kinder eyes, as though the job hadn't started to quell his joy for life yet. Perhaps someone you could trust and the sort of policeman you'd want to be helping you if you were in trouble.

"I'd have liked to have kept seeing her. I thought it was going well."

"Did you ever argue?" he questioned.

"No, that was why I was a little surprised she wanted to end it."

"So…" the older one jumped in, as if he was bored with his colleague's line of questioning, "…can you remember where you were the night of her murder." He put emphasis on the word murder.

Maybe it was to make me understand the seriousness of the conversation. I'd been expecting this question but hadn't formulated a response beyond saying I couldn't remember. I knew this may not be good enough. I asked them to confirm the date, trying to buy time to think, as well as showing that I may not be able to remember.

"I'm not certain, but I think I was with my girlfriend," knowing it was a gamble as I said it.

"New girlfriend?" he replied, a little disbelieving, as if it was difficult to appreciate I could have another girlfriend so soon.

"Yes." I said in a way that suggested it was obvious.

"Can you give me her details please?"

I gave them Kez's name and sister's address, knowing it was more than possible she'd deny it. I'd acted rashly telling them this, had been panicked into it. As I was showing them out the door, I regretted not saying I'd been home alone that night. They clearly didn't have anything concrete on me, so I probably didn't need an alibi.

As I was about to shut the door, the older one turned around and said, what seemed as an afterthought, "We may need you to come down to the station for more questioning and to take a swab."

I wondered if he was saying this to put the wind up me and catch me off guard when I'd relaxed, now they were leaving.

"If necessary, of course," I replied.

"Oh, it may well be so." He turned away and walked off, his colleague behind giving me a last glance. He looked as though he was weighing up my reaction to this as well as what his senior colleague meant by it. I closed the door and did a ubiquitous puff of the cheeks. I needed to act fast, but without showing signs of guilt. I doubt they had my phone tapped, but they may follow me. It was half an hour before I phoned Kez. I'd spent that time purely analysing the conversation with the police and how I'd reacted. I thought overall I'd done OK, not bringing suspicion upon myself, but and it was a big but, providing Kez helped me. It was positive that they hadn't mentioned the other killings. One thing that did puzzle me was that it had been quite some time since I'd mowed down my ex and it seemed strange that it had taken them so long to get round to questioning me if it was routine, which it had certainly come across as. Although, if they had a lead on me, surely they would have taken a less casual approach.

Annoyingly, there was no answer from Kez. I left a message saying to call me as soon as she could. I didn't want to sound too panicked, but hoped she'd pick up that it was important. Given I hadn't returned her last call, she may well not bother. If I didn't hear back from her, I'd need to see her in person. I was reluctant to do this straight away but decided I should do it by the end of the day. I had to beat my two new law upholding friends to it. I did nothing for the rest of the day, except continue to analyse the interview to the point it was driving me mad. How would I cope if it got serious? The evening came and I decided to seek out Kez. I had to try to catch up with her even if I was being followed by the police. After all, in their eyes, she was my girlfriend, so it would be normal to go and see her.

Knocking on her door, I was relieved to see movement inside. It concerned me that she might be away, which wouldn't help my cause. She answered the door and immediately smiled when she saw me. I recognised it as almost a satisfying one that meant she was happy I'd come running to her. She didn't have self-esteem issues, that was for sure. However, I was content to muscle her ego if she did what I wanted. Sitting on her sofa, she offered me a beer, which I gladly accepted. She handed it to me and sat opposite in an armchair.

Before I had a chance to start talking, she said, "I bet I can guess what this is about."

"I doubt that." I replied, thinking how she was going to react.

"Try me," she responded.

"OK." I said, realising I might as well humour her.

"I think that earlier today you were visited by two cops, who were asking you questions about your ex. One of them was where you were on the night she was killed." I was stunned and probably looked it as she sat there grinning in between taking swigs of her beer. "Am I right?" she said in a patronising way that a parent might ask a child. More recently, despite her stunning good looks, there were times when I would have liked to punch Kez. Her self-satisfying ways were incredibly annoying and very much behind my decision to not return her call.

Eventually, I smiled, "How do you know?"

"Well, earlier today, the same two cops paid me a visit."

"Christ, they didn't hang about."

"No, not at all." She paused after this. I knew she wanted me to ask what they had said and to looked panicked. Indeed, I was nervous, my heart was beating fast. I took a swig of my beer.

"What did they ask you?"

"They asked about our relationship and more specifically where you were that night." Again, she paused for effect.

I played the game she wanted me to and asked, "What did you say?"

"I said, since I'd known you, that you'd turned into a hit man, albeit an amateur one, and that that night you weren't with me, you were busy running over your ex."

I laughed, trying to hide how nervous I was. "What did you really say, Kez?"

She took a swig of beer and looked at me. "Of course, I told them you were here. Although you've got a nerve. Firstly, for calling me your girlfriend and secondly for assuming I'd help you out. You're lucky I have a hatred for all police. Don't do anything like that again without asking me," she said, reprimanding me. I inwardly felt relief. That had been close. Kez's annoyance, which seemed genuine, didn't bother me. That was just her way of trying to maintain the power in our strange relationship.

"Sorry, and thanks. I owe you big time." I said, once again playing along with her.

"You certainly do. It's becoming a habit these days," she replied, maintaining her sternness.

Now that I had ascertained I was in the clear, as far as my alibi was concerned, I was keen to get out of there, not harbouring any desire to stay in Kez's company longer than I had to.

"So, what next then?" she asked me whilst I was wondering how quickly I could escape.

"What do you mean?"

"Well, the police are on to you. One statement from me isn't going to put you in the clear. They're not stupid. They know full well that I could be lying."

"Yes, true, but I don't think they have anything else on me, judging by their questions. If they had hard evidence I wouldn't be sitting here now. The only thing I can't work out was why they have come to me now. It's been a while, so if I was part of their routine enquiries surely they would have paid me a visit a while ago."

"Hmmm." Kez muttered pensively.

I was just about to make my excuses and leave when she spoke again. "Did you ever follow up on those details I gave you?"

"Yes, I did track them a bit, but I didn't gain anything concrete from it, so I gave up."

"So, you're going to carry on doing what they ask you to are you?"

"Well, I'm not sure they'll ask me to do anything else. I wasn't paid for my last job."

"Really?" Kez, took the last drink from her beer and stared at the ceiling. "What do you think that means?" she said with genuine curiosity. I knew she had always been fascinated with my illegal profession, but she did seem to be showing interest beyond that.

"No idea." I said, "but I do know that should I get another job, I'm not doing it," I replied, impressed with my own bravado. I got up.

"Thanks for the beer and helping me out."

Kez nodded and walked with me to the door.

"I think you need to watch yourself," she said.

"Yeah, maybe, but I don't think I'll hear from them again."

"I wouldn't be so sure," she replied. I met her eyes as she said this, she quickly looked away. Something about the way she'd said it alarmed me. Things started to click in my mind.

"You know more about all this, don't you?"

"No," she said firmly, but I could tell she was lying. This infuriated me. I knew she liked to play her games, but this was a different level. Before I knew it, I had pushed her about against the wall.

"Tell me what you know," I shouted, my face close against hers. For the first time that I'd known her, I saw her look afraid. Even though I knew it wasn't right being aggressive with her, this pleased me.

"I don't know anything else," she said, trying to escape my grip on her shoulders. Whilst Kez wasn't small and appeared fit, I could easily overpower her. I could tell she was going to give in, so I continued to hold her there.

"OK. I'll tell you what else I know. Just let me go." She walked away, clearly pissed off. I thought about pulling her back but decided to give her a moment. She went into the kitchen. I sat back down on the sofa, trying to calm myself. Shortly afterwards, she emerged, holding a lit cigarette. She had the packet in her other hand and offered me one. I took it and she gave me hers to light it with. She sat back down on her armchair. She took another drag of her cigarette before she spoke.

"The police were tipped off about you," she said, seemingly calmer now.

"What? By who?" I asked confused.

"Those guys, the ones I gave you the address of."

"How do you know?"

"My friend, the one who tracked them with me, he kind of knows them," she said, pulling heavily again on her cigarette.

"Why didn't you tell me?" This was the first of many questions I had in my head that I put into speech.

"It's complicated, but I wanted to lead you to find out yourself," she said, eyeing me. I felt she was trying to gauge my reaction to this news.

"That's bullshit, Kez. What's complicated and why couldn't you have least told me that the police had been tipped off about me?"

"My friend, he's, well, compromised. If it was found out he was helping you, he'd be in trouble."

"OK," I said, deciding to give up on this part. "How do you know they'd tipped me off and why would they do that?"

"Well, he's sort of acquainted with them." She paused, this time not to play for effect, but to take another drag of her rapidly diminishing cigarette. "They want to take you out of the game was how it was explained to me. I don't know exactly, but it sounds like they have finished with their need for you. You saying you weren't paid for that last job seems to back that up."

I started to feel the anger rising again. Although she was telling me what she knew, there was more to this, and I felt frustrated even if she was telling me everything she'd been told.

"What are the names of these two guys and how many others are there?"

She looked at me, clearly deciding whether she could get away with not telling me.

"Don't make me have to do this the hard way." I said.

"I only know one of their names. Dave McKendrick. I don't know what his sidekick is called. There are probably also a couple of hangers on in their crowd, but I think they are the main two."

"How does your mate know them?"

She sighed. "If it gets out I've told you this, I'm in deep shit." I didn't think she was looking for sympathy, but I certainly wasn't going to give her any. "All I know is that he occasionally crosses their path in his dealings," she continued. "It goes without saying they're not very nice people."

"Any idea why they've finished with me?"

"No," she said emphatically, "I've no idea about what they were getting you to do and I don't think my friend has. All he knew is that they seem to want you out the picture and that maybe putting you in the frame was an easy way of doing it."

I left after this, convinced that she'd told me all she knew. I at least had a name that I could follow up on. But I was very worried. If the police left me alone, then these guys could well come after me. Either outcome was bad.

Over the next twenty-four hours, I thought about my limited options. I could run away, but that would certainly make me look guilty in the eyes of the police, meaning I could probably never return. I decided I had to tackle the problem. If I was to do that, I needed to act quickly.

I sought out Brad. I hadn't seen him too many times since he'd put me in touch with Jason. A lot had happened since then.

On the handful of occasions I had seen him, he'd tried to find out more about what happened with the gun, but I'd always steered him off the subject without giving anything away. Now I was going to start his questioning all over again. I phoned and arranged to meet him in the Crooked Billet. He'd know it was more than just a social drink as we never pre-arranged our meetings, but I didn't want to wait until our next chance encounter. I thought about what I'd tell him. I knew I wouldn't get away with being as aloof as last time. I got there early and bought him a beer whilst I was waiting. He walked in slightly later than agreed. I handed him his beer and we exchanged small talk for a couple of minutes.

It wasn't long before he questioned me. "So, what's all this about? You've got me worried. You don't need anything more for your arsenal?" he said, half joking.

"I've got a name that I need you to run by your darker acquaintances. See what they can find out," I said, getting straight to the point.

"Go on?" He replied.

"Dave McKendrick."

Brad took a sip of his beer and furrowed his beer. "That name rings a bell. Where do I know it from?" Then his expression turned to that of concern. "Why are you asking? What's going on with you, mate? First the gun, then you keep disappearing and now this."

"I know, I've got myself into a bit of trouble and this guy seems to have it in for me."

"What sort of trouble?" There was genuine concern in his voice. I felt bad and thought, if only he knew. The truth wasn't an option.

"Let's say it's partly financial," I said, knowing this wouldn't completely placate him.

"How, why have you been borrowing from villains? Christ, mate, I'm not loaded, but you could come to me first. I could help you or at least find someone who won't kneecap you if you miss a payment."

"I didn't want to get mates involved," I said, realising the irony of my statement.

"Or what's wrong with Barclays? I always thought you were quite astute, but you seem to be losing your marbles."

"Look, let's just say I got myself involved with the wrong type of girl. You're right, I've been stupid, but I want to put it straight."

"What girl and what have you been buying, other than guns? Also, how are you going to put it straight other than pay them back?"

"Mate, it's for the best I don't tell you more. I don't want you involved. Well, any more than doing me this one favour. I need to know who exactly he is and also, I think he has a main sidekick. Anything you can find out about him would be good as well." I took a sip of my beer, inwardly praying Brad would help me rather than just lecture me.

"Of course I will, but you've got to sort yourself out. None of this adds up, it's like I don't know you anymore. Promise me you'll go back on the straight and narrow once this is over. If you escape in one piece," he added as an afterthought.

"I will, mate. Believe you me, there's nothing more I want than to get back to a normal life. When do you think you can get the information?"

"I'm in work tomorrow. I'll do some digging then."

"Thanks, mate. I owe you big time."

We had a few more beers, but the previous conversation

hung over the night. I could tell Brad hadn't stopped thinking about it and felt a bit betrayed I hadn't come to him earlier or told him more. Despite this, I knew he would help me. It was in his nature to. I was also confident that he'd be able to find something out. These gangs tended to know about each other, from what I could gather. I just had to nervously wait. I was permanently thinking about receiving a visit from either the police or some thugs.

Fortunately for me, another lorry driving job came up the next day and once again I hit the road for a couple of days, happy to escape home and the impending dangers that I felt around it. It didn't stop me thinking about it, though. My hope was to find out enough information about Dave and his mate to see if I could do a hit on them. There may be more of them, but from what Kez said, they ran the show and therefore if I eliminated them, it should stop everything.

There was a message from Brad when I returned. He wanted to meet. I hoped he had good information for me. We sat in a smaller, quieter pub that we didn't normally frequent, so we wouldn't be interrupted by any of our other mates and drinking friends.

"It's what I thought," he said looking troubled. "Dave McKendrick and his partner Jon Bridge are two of the nastiest pieces of work in the manor. I'm not sure you know what you've got yourself into. Even some of the toughest guys I spoke to wouldn't get involved with them"

"I know it's bad. Tell me more."

"Well, they deal. This isn't what it's about is it?"

"Drugs?" I questioned.

"Yeah, you're not dealing, are you? Taking their business. From what I hear they don't take too kindly to that."

I shook my head, hoping Brad would keep telling me information rather than asking me questions.

"They've both done time, GBH, that sort of thing. From what I understand, they generally get other people to do their dirty work."

"Where do they hang out; did you find out anything like that?" I asked. He looked confused.

"Do you want to find them?" he said incredulously. "I thought you wanted to avoid them, not present them with a chance to permanently damage you."

"Yes and no. I might need to face the music at some point and working out where and when is best the place to do it would help."

"What exactly have you done to upset them?" Brad asked.

"I told you it's financial."

"Can you pay them back?"

"I'm working on it. Do you know anything else?" I said, trying not to show how impatient I was feeling.

"They are quite often in the snooker club, the one on Banks Street. They may even have a stake in it, I was told. You can probably find them there on a regular basis." This was useful information, at least.

"Thanks, Brad. I appreciate your help."

"If there's anything I can do. I've got a little bit of cash put away. Not much, but I'll lend it to you if it will help." He had a heart of gold.

"Thanks, mate, you're a diamond, but I'm going to sort this out myself."

"OK. Oh, I remembered one last thing I was told. McKendrick recently had a big bust up with one of his cousins who was involved with them before. Normally this cousin of his would have been in hospital by now, but as he's family he's off the hook. Apparently, there's bad blood there and they hate each other with a passion."

"Interesting. Do you know what caused it?"

"No idea," Brad replied.

"What's his name?" I could see by Brad's expression he regretted what he was telling me.

"Don't think about getting involved in that. It would make things ten times worse."

"I know, but it would be good to know for back up. You know if all else fails."

"Jim, same surname."

We once again parted with Brad showing concern about my welfare and what I was up to.

I spent the next few days watching the snooker club. It was in a rundown area and I didn't like hanging around there much. But Brad was right, they were there regularly. My round the clock surveillance also told me they often left there late at night or in the early hours of the morning. The entrance was secluded and overlooked by a derelict block of flats that might present a good opportunity to carry out one potential plan. I also did some digging on Jim McKendrick. I found out he ran a pub that I had very occasionally been in and I wondered whether I should seek him out. It was risky, seeing as Dave was family, but if what Brad said was true then he might be willing to assist me. One good bit of news was that the police had not returned since their initial visit. But I was aware that although this might mean I was out of the frame with my ex-girlfriend at the moment, McKendrick and co. might be looking for other ways to get rid of me. I did another lorry job which came up, happy once again to be away. I knew once I returned, I had to act before it became too late.

When I returned, I went to the Red Lion pub. God knows why I'd ever drunk there before. It was run down and only frequented by a few downbeat locals spending their dole money in the best way they knew how to. I sat at the bar, slowly sipping my pint whilst smoking. I'd received a couple of strange looks, but nothing threatening. After a couple of pints, I struck up a conversation with the bar maid. She was friendly enough and I felt sorry for her working there. She was probably in her forties and I guessed needed the money to support her family.

"Is the owner, Jim, around tonight?" I asked, trying to keep my voice at a level that no one else would hear. The lack of atmosphere in the pub was heightened by a jukebox laying redundant in the corner, possibly out of order. Her manner instantly became suspicious and defensive.

"No, do you know him?" she replied, slightly nervous, probably under instructions of how to respond to such questions from people she hadn't seen before.

"OK, not to worry," I responded, playing down the matter. She drifted to the other end of the bar and I got some more curious looks from the few depressed-looking punters. I ordered another pint, keeping myself to myself whilst drinking it. Later, as I left, I thanked the bar maid and told her to tell Jim I was keen to meet him, giving her my name and phone number. She once again looked nervous, but nodded in agreement. I made my way home, down beat that I hadn't made progress.

Chapter Twelve

I woke with a start, something I'd done a few times recently, always thinking there was someone in my flat. Could this be the one time there really was? My luminous clock said the time was 3.43 a.m. My senses came alive, trying to detect sounds and movement, my heartbeat increasing like a sports car going from nought to sixty. A noise; was that inside or outside? I got out of bed, grabbing the gun on my bed side table. I made my way to the door and listened. I'd thought through a few times what I'd do in this situation: wait behind the door for them to come in and shoot. It was possible that it might be a burglar, but I couldn't take the chance. The likelihood was that it was someone who wanted to do me serious harm. It seemed like I was waiting there for ages, whilst the intruder searched the rest of the flat. I couldn't be sure, but there only sounded like one. It seemed obvious to me which one would be the bedroom, so I didn't understand why it was taking so long. Maybe they were checking that nobody else was staying in the living room. Then, finally, when I thought perhaps they were leaving or I'd imagined it all, the door handle moved. I took a deep breath. I'd done this six times now; it shouldn't be a problem. They slowly moved into the room. My bedroom was very dark, being at the back of the flat where there was no street light penetrating through the curtains. My vision was at its highest for seeing the dark, having been asleep for a few hours. An advantage I'd have over my intruder. I'd read somewhere that for the eyes to fully adjust to darkness can take up to a couple of hours. I raised the gun, ready to fire as soon as it was pointed at their head. I lined it up, but just as I was about to put pressure on the trigger, I thought that perhaps I should make them talk first, find out more about what was going on and who they were. This hesitation cost me. In that moment, they sensed I was there and lashed out, a forearm to my neck which pushed me back against the wall. I brought my arm down against the wall to keep my balance, meaning I was no longer aiming the gun at the target. Before I knew it, we were grappling with each other and the gun fell to the floor. I could now make out the silhouette of a thick-set man who was larger than me; he held a knife. I concentrated on restricting the movement of the arm of the hand he held it in. It was like a strange wrestling match and neither of us could reach any advantageous position over the other. Because I had all my strength restraining his arm with the knife, I was unable to strike a blow to him. I decided to take a gamble. With one movement, I released his arm and darted to my left, narrowly avoiding the instant lunge he made with the knife. I sent a left hook to the side of his head, the connection not as well timed as I wanted. However, this gave me enough time to land a blow to his midriff, winding him. I then shoved him backwards and he fell to the floor, dropping the knife in the process. I leapt on top of him and punched him hard in the face.

"Who are you, who sent you?" I shouted. There was no response and I hit him again before asking the same questions. He started wriggling and managed to gain enough momentum that he shoved me off. I fell backwards and as I did, I fell onto the gun. He was getting up and I quickly grabbed the gun. I could see him making to kick me whilst I was on the floor. I fired the gun before I had time to aim it properly, more to shock him than harm him. Even though the silencer was on, it was clear what the noise was, and this sent him scampering out of the door. I got up and followed him, but he was quick and had covered the ground from my bedroom down the hallway corridor and out of the door before I could take good aim at him. I stood in the hallway, gun in hand, heart beating fast and out of breath. I waited like that for a couple of minutes. I knew he wasn't coming back, but I didn't want to take the risk. Eventually I shut the door, noticing the broken lock, and went and sat down. That had been close. I couldn't stay here any longer.

I packed some things. I was going to leave immediately and check into a hotel later that day. Staying with a friend or family wasn't an option. I didn't want to bring anybody I knew into this. As I walked out of the flat, I noticed a piece of paper that must have been put through the door, perhaps after I went to bed and I hadn't seen it in all the commotion earlier. I grabbed it without reading it. I was still shaken up and didn't want to hang around any longer than I needed to.

Later that day, lying on the bed in my small hotel room, I unfolded the piece of paper. All it said was "Jim" and a phone number. It had been a bad day and the pokey, depressing hotel room I'd checked myself into didn't help. I needed to sort everything out, which wasn't going to be easy. At least Jim might be able to help me. I didn't want to get my hopes up though.

I found a phone box a short distance from the hotel and made the call. He instantly came across as blunt and aggressive. Once I introduced myself, he responded. "So, why do you want to speak to me. What do you want?"

"I want to talk about Dave, your cousin," I answered, hoping this might get him interested enough to say yes.

"What about him?"

"I think we might be able to help each other," I said,

gambling he might like this line of thought.

"How?" He barked back. This wasn't easy, I thought.

"I think we might have a common interest in bringing him down a peg or two." I winced as I completed the sentence. It was quiet for a few seconds. I held my breath, waiting for him to respond.

"Come to the pub later. But you better not be wasting my time." With that, the line went dead. I stepped out of the phone box. Not easy, but at least I'd made progress. Now I needed to work out what strategy I would take when I saw him. He wasn't going to be easy to please.

I arrived at the pub later that evening. The same barmaid was serving, and it felt like a similar type of clientele were in there too. Before I could even order a pint, the barmaid had ushered me round the bar and up some stairs. She showed me through a door, and I was greeted with the sight of what I assumed was Jim, laying casually on a sofa watching television. He looked tall, even from a lounging position. He was a bit younger than I'd assumed, maybe even the right side of thirty. His bright ginger hair was prominent on his head. He looked through narrow greyish-green eyes and nodded towards an armchair, puffing on a cigarette as he did so. I sat down and waited for him to speak. He surveyed me for a few seconds and then said, "What you got that's so interesting."

"I know someone who's fallen out with Dave and wants to put the frighteners on him." Jim sniggered at this.

"In what way?" he replied.

"Shake him up a bit, you know, so he learns a lesson." Jim laughed again, louder this time.

"Good luck to him. Anyway, where do I come in?"

"Well, I understood you're not the best of mates at the

moment. He'd like to know a bit more about him and ways that he could get to him."

"Maybe you're right. Dave and I did have a falling out, but I ain't offering a free service to someone else who's landed on the wrong side of him. Especially someone I don't know."

I knew from our brief phone call he may be difficult.

"So, you don't want to help. In that case, there's no point in wasting any more of our time," I said, standing up to leave.

"Let's cut the crap first," he said as I was about to walk out of the door. I'd hoped this bluff would work. I looked at him and he motioned for me to sit back down. I did as I was told.

"We need to be honest with each other. It's obviously you that has the issue with Dave." I'd been unsure of this plan to begin with; I wrongly thought it might make it less personal and therefore he'd help me if he thought he didn't know the person who was after Dave.

"OK." I agreed.

"If you want to get at him, you need to do a proper job. Dave doesn't let grudges go, so if you don't complete the job, it will come back to haunt you." We were getting somewhere now.

"I had a similar thought," I said. At this point, I caught movement out of the corner of my eye, by the door. I looked up and was shocked to see Kez walk into the room. It threw me for a moment, rendering me speechless. She sat next to Jim and cuddled up to him, smiling at me. My initial surprise dissipated as she did this and as I thought it through things made a bit more sense. Kez had got her information from Jim. They continued looking at me. I was sure they wanted me to be shocked and ask questions, but I remained silent, thinking back through my conversations with Kez. I thought they had been playing me. Pushing me towards Dave to do their dirty work. Finally, Jim spoke.

"I can get you into the club where you can wait for them," he said. I nodded a response, but my mind was racing. What if McKendrick had nothing to do with setting my jobs and I was just being used? It was difficult to know what to do, but I had to try to find out more to be sure.

"It will cost you, though," he continued. This bit threw me even more. Now he was demanding money for the information. I didn't like it one bit

"How do I know Dave is my man?" I asked, ignoring the money part for now. Jim scowled, but after a couple of seconds broke into a smile. Kez's expression didn't change, an annoying self-satisfied look on her face.

"Believe what you like. You're the one who came to me for help," he said. As though as an afterthought, he added, "You're the one at risk if you do nothing."

I felt anger rising within me, driven by the frustration of not being able to verify the truth, of not being in control, Kez looking smug and Jim acting all superior. Knowing I was acting rashly, I pulled the gun from my coat pocket. "Right, it's about time we got to the truth. If McKendrick is connected to my hits, you need to prove it." Kez, looked mildly alarmed to find the gun pointing in her direction, but Jim remained passive, his expression neutral. Between them they didn't respond.

"I'm serious," I shouted.

Jim rolled his eyes, signalling he was bored with this. "What do you mean by hits?" he said.

"Let's not play games. You know what I mean."

"You can play the big man as much as you like, pointing that gun at me, but I don't know anything about hits." I studied him. He seemed genuine, but I couldn't be certain. I looked at Kez;

she had a blank expression on her face that gave nothing away.

"If that's the case, what interest am I to him?"

"I don't know. You should know better than me. You've obviously upset him somehow. Although, it doesn't take much in my experience."

I felt frustration again. Every time it seemed I was getting closer to the truth, I received a setback. If Jim did know nothing about it—although I certainly couldn't be sure he was telling the truth—then that was another lead gone. Of course, that could mean that McKendrick wasn't the perpetrator behind my hits. If this was the case, then why was he upset with me? I gave up and accepted Jim's word, feeling that I wasn't going to make more progress by threatening him. As if to at least back up he was on my side, Jim did give me a key to McKendrick's club and the code to the alarm. He said they had an office at the back. If I broke in one night, I could lie in wait for them. They would be there most lunchtimes. He also dropped his request for money which felt like a moral victory on my part. I left him and Kez there, Kez back to her grinning self once I'd put the gun away. Jim warned me that if I ever pointed a gun at him again, I'd better shoot him, as I wouldn't survive afterwards. Big man stuff that I expected and was starting to become immune to. He also told me that if I took out Dave and his sidekick, there shouldn't be any more trouble. Easy in principle, but my toughest assignment yet.

Back in my hotel room, I considered my options. It occurred to me I should maybe try speaking to Kez on her own. There was a chance she might tell me more now I knew about her and Jim. It pains me to admit it, but I wanted to see her again. I realised afterwards that I was looking for signs she was still on my side. The next day I went to see her, but she was out. She was probably still with Jim. I would try again a couple of days later. She wasn't the sort of person who stayed in the same place for long. That night in my hotel room, I started planning how I would take out McKendrick. Even if he wasn't involved in my work, I believed he was after me and felt I had to get to him first. I didn't like the idea of breaking in overnight and waiting. I don't think Jim had thought it through. I needed them there on their own, I couldn't take them out whilst punters were playing snooker in the club. What I did think I'd do was check out their office one night to see if I could find anything interesting.

I waited until the next Monday when it should be quiet, and made my way over there in the early hours of the morning. The key and alarm code were good, and I was in with no problems at all. I found the office, but annoyingly it was locked. This wasn't going to deter me, and I forced my way in, not bothered about the fact it would be noticed the next day. Their office was nice. Expensive television, drinks cabinet that was fully stocked and some good plush furniture. I helped myself to some whisky that looked expensive. It made me feel good to be there, helping myself to their stocks. I then started looking around, not sure what I may find. I tried some drawers first, but found nothing of interest, only finances and bills. I then came across a drawer that was locked. It wasn't easy to prise open, but with a bit of physical persuasion I got in. There were papers in there, but nothing of interest to me. Underneath that, I found a wad of twenty-pound notes and a revolver. I was going to gratefully take both of those. I was enjoying it here, taking advantage of the goodies McKendrick and co. had left me. Lastly, at the bottom of the drawer I found a disc. I pocketed this as well.

After this I decided to get out, happy with my findings. I hadn't found out much more, but I had the disc and wondered whether this would tell me anything. It wasn't until I was back in my hotel room that I realised I had no way of watching it. There wasn't a DVD player in my room, and I wasn't going to risk going back to my place. I'd decided I should stay clear of there until this was over. I didn't think it would provide the answers I really wanted, given the conversation I'd had with Jim, but at the least it may give something juicy about McKendrick and his mates. I could take it to someone I knew, but I may not want them to see what was on there. In the end, the only option I could think of was to buy a cheap DVD player and connect it up to the TV in my room. The next day I bought one and, having connected it, I inserted the disc and sat on the edge of my bed, eagerly waiting to see what was going to be on there. I was disappointed. It turned out to be amateur footage of a dodgy nature, probably with one of McKendrick's girlfriends. I realised how optimistic I'd been that the disc would somehow provide me with good information on the McKendricks and even their involvement with me. I'd got no further in that respect. On top of that, I felt time was running out. I decided I'd check out Kez one last time before I acted. I knew it was a little risky, as they probably knew I was connected to her. Also, she might still be at Jim's, but I felt it was worth a try. I showed up at her door, not holding out much hope of her answering, with there being no sign of her car. To my surprise, the door opened shortly after I knocked, but I was greeted not by Kez, but another woman. We both looked at each other blankly for a moment.

"Is Kez in?" I asked, not hiding the confusion in my voice.

"No," came a blunt reply that had an element of "who are you?" to it. I introduced myself and to my surprise she knew me.

"Oh, I've been wanting to meet you," she said, which took me aback a little.

"Are you her sister?" I asked.

"Yes, I think I know where she is," she replied.

"Oh, good," I said, fully expecting to be told she was with Jim.

"She's at the local pub, with one of her mates," she said pointing down the street. So, she wasn't with Jim. I thanked her sister. I'd have preferred to have spoken to Kez on her own, but I didn't know when I'd get another opportunity. I walked into the pub. It was relatively busy. I saw Kez sitting at a table on one side. Opposite her was a guy. He had his back to me, but it didn't appear to be anyone I knew. For some reason, I was expecting her to be with another girl, which, retrospectively, I realised was naive. This wasn't going to deter me. I bought myself a pint and stood at the bar a few minutes, supping it and smoking a cigarette. Then I wondered over to where she was. They were chatting away but I had no issues with interrupting them.

"Hi, Kez," I said standing over them.

"Oh, hello," she replied, looking surprised to see me.

"We need to talk," I said. The guy she was with looked like he didn't know how to react to my sudden appearance.

"Go ahead." Kez said.

"In private." I demanded, knowing full well she knew I'd meant this to begin with.

"Well, I'm a little busy at the moment," she said nodding her head to her companion.

"Well, I can wait." I responded pulling up a chair and placing my beer on the table.

"Oh! for Christ's sake," Kez sighed. "You're becoming a right pain in the arse." She looked at her watch and, without consulting her drinking partner, said, "Give me fifteen minutes."

"OK." I said, standing up and taking my beer from the table. Before I could ask where I should wait, she told me, like a parent talking to a naughty child, to wait at the bar. I did as I was told, pleased I'd got my way. I didn't look over towards them again. Although, she obviously sent the guy packing because she was with me shortly afterwards. I felt sorry for him. Probably another guy she was leading a merry dance.

"You don't care for female company much, do you?" I said to her.

"What do you want?" she said impatiently, ignoring my question.

"How did you get rid of him?"

"You're beginning to piss me off. Now tell me what you want or I'm leaving."

"I want to know what's going on, Kez." She let out a loud sigh at this. "Don't pretend you've told me everything. Every time I see you, I learn more, so there's bound to be things you haven't told me."

"There's things I can't tell you," she said. I could tell she was braver as we were in public. It would have been better to have spoken to her at home where I would have had a greater chance of extracting more from her.

"What can you tell me? Was Jim telling the truth?"

"I don't think he was lying to you. All I can say is, things might not be as they seem," she said, looking briefly as though she may feel sorry for me. Not that this was any less ambiguous.

"I understand you can't say much, but I'm at a loss as to what this is all about," I said softly, trying to take advantage of her moment of weakness, away from her normal cold demeanour.

"Sorry, I can't help you anymore," she said, looking regretful, but then added, as if to eradicate any guilt she was feeling, "You got yourself into this, you need to find a way out of it." With this she went, and with it what felt like my last hope of finding out what I was involved in. I nursed my pint at the bar, feeling sorry for myself. I'd been delaying my plan, but not for any longer. I was nervous and excited about what lay ahead.

During one of my previous lorry jobs, I'd taken my rifle and found somewhere where I could practice. After hitting Peter first time, I'd wondered if I'd been lucky or not. I didn't want to assume I'd be so accurate the next time. The practice was good, and I was happy with my aim. I'd been to the flats opposite the snooker club a couple of times to check out vantage points. They were fenced off, but they weren't too difficult to penetrate. I was pretty sure that I wasn't the only one breaking in there. I'd heard noises and suspected there were other people in there, such as squatters or druggies. They were due to be destroyed soon, but I imagined slow administration or lack of funding by the council had delayed it

The first three nights that I kept vigil over the club, only one of McKendrick or his sidekick appeared. I wanted to do the job in one go. On the fourth night, I saw them both arrive around ten thirty and enter the club. What I hadn't expected was to see Kez walk in there with them. She never failed to amaze me. It made me think more about her role in all this. She seemed to be in cahoots with all sides. I also thought about when we were in the pub together a few days earlier. She'd been cryptic about what was going on. I felt angry that I had been duped. Although she had helped me, I had no idea what other lies she had spun me or what she was doing behind my back.

Knowing they'd be in there a couple of hours at least, I went and got something to eat and fetched the rifle. I only wanted to carry it into the flats when I knew I was going to use it. The flats had an eerie feel to them, remnants of an unpleasant place to live and many wrongdoings that had occurred there when they were frequented. There were occasional noises from one of the other illegal occupants. It certainly added to the tension I was feeling that was further exacerbated by knowing that everything was coming to a head. I'd allowed myself to think about what I'd do if I came out of this successfully. It was certainly going to be difficult going back to a normal life. My recent experiences would undoubtedly taint my views on things going forward. Bigger issues were immediate as I waited for McKendrick and co. to come out. I was hoping they'd exit together. I was on the third floor because of its good vantage point, but also as it was a relatively quick exit away.

It must have been after two in the morning when the door opened, and his sidekick appeared, followed by a couple of the others. Just as I was concerned McKendrick was remaining in there, he also appeared. Perfect for me, they hung around outside chatting. There were six of them. I lined up McKendrick through the sight, I was now in the zone, a world of my own, a place I was beginning to enjoy being. I was as calm as I had been all night. I squeezed the trigger. The time between this and the bullet hitting seemed to move in slow motion. He fell to the floor immediately and I knew I had success. This was where I needed to be quick, as panic set in around the fallen body. I couldn't get a good sight of his sidekick. I had thought about this and was prepared to sacrifice one or two of the others to ensure I got the job done. However, there was something that had broken my deep focus on the job. Like trying to block out a disturbance whilst sleeping, I ignored it briefly, but eventually I was forced to turn around before I fired another shot. Standing six feet away from me, but dead still, was a hooded man. He was staring straight at me. I couldn't make out his features well in the gloom, but he looked a deathly figure. By the time I looked back at the club, McKendrick's so called friends were scampering away, leaving him for dead. Some were probably running for their lives. It was possible one or two might try to find me. I had to get out of there quickly. I stood up; the hooded guy looked confused and dazed, as if not knowing to believe what he saw. He'd probably had many illusions before, judging by the state of him. I grabbed my rifle and the bag I carried it in. I pushed past him; his expression changed to that of fear, but he didn't move. As I made my way down the graffiti ridden stairs that had a urine stench, I heard sirens coming towards the area. I reached the first floor and I looked over to where I had parked my car. I thought I saw people milling around it. What if McKendrick's gang had found it and were waiting there? It was at that point that I'd realised that in my rush to get away, I'd left my gun upstairs. That hooded guy had thrown me. It annoyed me that something small had distracted me. I stood there for a few seconds, working out what to do. Going back for it would lose time; they may have worked out where I had fired from, and the police would be all around here soon. But if there were a couple of McKendrick's crew that had found my car and were lying in wait, I'd need a gun. Just having the rifle wasn't good enough. I turned and ran back upstairs, thinking as I did it whether I should just leave my car once I was out of the flats and get back to the hotel another way. The sirens were loud now and occasionally I could see a blue light coming through the glass-less windows of the dereliction. I entered the area, or former flat, where I'd fired from. I knew exactly where I'd left it, and had pictured how I would grab it and run back out. As I got there, standing there like he was last time, but this time facing the opposite way, was the same guy, the hooded man. I stopped and stared. This time he had a different look; in fact, he was grinning inanely and then I realised why. He was holding my gun and it was pointed at me. I was weighing up how serious he may be, as well as if he had any chance of hitting me when he shouted.

"Money, give me your money!"

Before I had a chance to react, there was a noise and I realised he'd fired it. Relieved that he'd missed, I dived out the way and took cover behind a nearby wall that would have separated the rooms of the derelict flat we were in. I couldn't believe this was happening. I could hear him staggering towards me, muttering. I was trapped in a corner with nowhere to go. If I stayed where I was, even he wouldn't be able to miss once I was in his sights. I had to take a risk. I waited until I could hear him closer. I jumped out, running towards him as fast as I could. My plan worked as he was stunned and too slow to react. I tackled him rugby style to the floor, putting the aggression I felt into the contact I made with him. He went down hard, the chemicals he had taken preventing him from breaking his fall. I heard the gun fall to the floor. I landed on top of him and immediately got up. I gave him a quick kick to the head to ensure he stayed down. I then started looking for the gun in the gloom. Fortunately, it hadn't moved far and I located it within a few seconds. By this time he was trying to get to his feet. As he did, I crashed the gun down onto the back of his head. He collapsed again and I was sure he would stay down for a while now. I grabbed the bag my rifle was in and ran out. As I went back down the stairs, I thought about what my next move would be. Should I head for my car or away on foot? I'd need to avoid McKendrick's gang as well as any police that had arrived in the area. Once again, I looked out over towards my car from the vantage point by the stairs. There were still some people by it and they were standing out of the shadows this time. I stared harder and made out three men. I studied them for a while. McKendrick's sidekick, Bridge, always wore a cap when I saw him. He was of short, stocky build and I was sure I could make him out. They must be waiting for me and, despite my initial cynicism about their loyalty, looking for revenge. This was too good an opportunity to miss. It was highly risky though. The police were probably crawling all over the place by now, so I needed to escape quickly. As I took the rifle out of the bag that I had hurriedly put away on my first time down the stairs, I wondered if I could take all three of them out. As I steadied myself with the gun, I saw they had moved closer together. They were in a huddle, perhaps discussing what they should do next. I lined up Bridge in the sight. I hadn't used it much, but it already felt like a good friend. The shot felt louder than I'd remembered before, maybe because I was in a more exposed position. I'd certainly hit him, and he went down, but I wasn't able to tell if it had been a fatal shot. The other two reacted quickly and I had no time to line either of them up before they were out of sight. It was time for me to move as well. The noise would certainly have got the presence of the local constabulary interested. I ran down the remaining stairs. The flats had been blocked off by mesh fencing. I'd found a way over it in an area that had been lowered slightly. Handy work done by other trespassing entrants, I suspected. I leapt over it, already having it in mind to turn left away from where my car was and into the estate further. I soon realised the error of my ways. Within seconds, I saw some police. I turned immediately, but not before they saw me. I looked just about as suspicious as possible. I was now sprinting away from where I'd seen them. I didn't look to see if they were giving chase but I assumed they were. The other problem I had was I was now running towards where the remainder of McKendrick's crew had last been. I knew I was in trouble; it was going to be hard to get away from both. It felt like a net was closing in around me. I was nearing my car now, hoping this was the better option. I removed the gun which I'd tucked inside my waist band. As I got to the car, I saw Bridge lying on the ground. There was blood coming from his mouth. I saw I had hit him in the neck. He looked up at me and made a gurgling noise. Fortunately, neither of his friends seemed to be in the immediate vicinity. Without thinking, I finished him off with a shot to the head. I opened the door of my car. As I jumped in, I saw a car screech up next to me. It wasn't a police car. At the same time, and from the behind the car, I saw two policemen running towards me, I felt encircled, almost paralysed, realising that my chances of escaping were limited. I had to try though; I couldn't talk my way out of it, that was for sure. I heard a noise from the car and noticed the back door open. I'd assumed it was related to McKendrick and expected to be shot at. Then I realised the noise was someone shouting at me from the front of the car.

"Get in!" I hesitated. The police were nearer. "Now!" he demanded. It was a gamble, but I did what I was told and leapt in. The car screeched away before I could even close the door. There were three men inside. I had never seen any of them before.

"Who are you?" I questioned.

The one in the back looked at me and smiled. "You've made quite a mess tonight," he said calmly, ignoring my question. He then relieved me of my gun and rifle. I sat back in the car as we drove fast through the streets.

Chapter Thirteen

It must have been nearly an hour before we stopped. I had not bothered to strike up conversation with them again, accepting I was at their mercy, but hopeful that they weren't going to do me any harm. We got out of the car. I was surprised they didn't try to tie me up or have hold of me. The thought occurred to me to run, but I had a feeling they would catch me. All three of them looked in good shape. Although not far out of the city, it was quieter as well as cooler, a different world from the council estate they had extracted me from. I was directed inside a smallish cottage, probably only two bedrooms, and given a cup of tea and a seat in the small lounge. Still nothing was said, although one of them was in the room at all times. I was then taken upstairs and shown a bedroom.

"Get some rest. We'll talk in the morning. You want to come out, knock." These were the only words said to me. The door was shut behind me and bolted, explaining the comment about knocking. It was a basic room, with a single bed and a cupboard. I laid on the bed, thinking I would never sleep. Although the adrenaline flow from earlier had abated, I still hadn't calmed down completely. I lay there, wondering who these people were.

I woke to the smell of bacon. Disoriented, I looked around to make out where I was. Sleep had come on fast, which was a surprise. My thoughts immediately returned to who these people were. Somehow, I felt comfortable with them, which would explain why I managed to sleep so well, but then logic defied this feeling. They must be after something, but I didn't know what. If they were going to hurt me then, I would have thought they would have done this by now. I lay there for a little longer, slowly mustering the energy to face the day. I knocked on the door. Almost immediately it was opened.

"Morning, nice to see you're finally in the land of the living." This said by the same guy who had been in the back of the car with me.

"Your exploits last night must have taken it out of you." I didn't like these references to what I did last night. Did they know that much and if so, how? I was still sure I'd not seen any of them before. I was led downstairs and into the kitchen where I was offered some of the delicious-smelling bacon and coffee. I enjoyed it, but not as much as I should have. I was waiting to find out the reason for being here, the apprehension reducing my taste bud senses. Silence remained whilst I ate, but again there was always one of them in the room.

I finished and remained seated there. I was now getting fed up with waiting. "When are we going to speak?" I asked.

The one in the room responded.

"Let's start now, if you've finished eating."

He led me through to a lounge and motioned for me to sit on the sofa. He sat on the other sofa and one of his colleagues was already there, sitting on a separate chair. It was strange how they were almost unnoticeable. Somehow, they blended into the background and their bland clothes and similar way of acting made them difficult to distinguish from each other. I was nervous but did not feel threatened and I had no idea what they were about to say.

"So," the one sitting on the armchair said, "you've made it through phase one."

"Phase one?" I repeated, questioning.

"Yes, now it's time to begin the second phase."

"What do you mean?" I asked.

"We're talking about what you've been doing over the last six months or so," the one on the chair interjected.

I felt more uncomfortable with this.

"Who are you?"

"We recruit killers. Our responsibility is to test, train and prepare."

"For what purpose?"

"National security." It was a blunt response that took me by surprise.

"You work for the government?" I tried to think through what he'd been saying, but it was difficult to take in. I had many questions floating around my head, which had been the case since the start of the exchange. Before I could formulate another, one of them spoke.

"It's an unusual method of recruitment, but we've had some success with the few trials we've completed, and it certainly has its advantages. Putting recruits through real life situations allows you to find out about them and what they are capable of. How they react to their first time, do they continue, does it become an addiction? Whilst you had some strange methods and possibly some luck, you showed the right appetite."

"But who was I killing?"

"That's irrelevant and not a good response. Assassins don't dwell on previous work." I laughed at this despite my annoyance at the answer. I didn't like where it was going, but at the same time realised it was at least an opportunity to find some answers to questions I'd been harbouring for a long time.

"Phase two starts with training and building on what you've learnt from phase one."

"So, you want me to kill more people?"

"Not until you've completed the programme."

"Hold on. What if I don't want to do it?" I asked, annoyed.

"Well, we're not going to forcefully make you do it." He replied. "But it was explained to you at the beginning that once you sign up, you're committed."

"So, I don't have an option? After all, you can't keep me locked up here if you want me to do more of your dirty work."

"You're perfectly free to go now."

"I am?"

"Except, there's no way of guaranteeing the police won't catch up with you for your misdemeanours, or that any villains you may have upset on the way won't come after you for revenge."

Their message was clear. It didn't appear I had a way out. I could run off abroad, but I had doubts I would even make it out of the country. Whilst I didn't like the fact I was effectively being bribed, I decided to explore more about what they were offering.

"So, what do I get out of this?"

"A new identity to delink you from the past, a job for life, oh, and you'll never have to worry about money again."

"How long will I have to do it for?"

"You're still a young man, so I think it's a bit early to be talking about retirement yet. However, as you get older and slower, we can review it, maybe put you into something less physical, before you enjoy a generous retirement package."

"Where will I live?"

"You can set up a home wherever you want for when you're off duty, yet we strongly recommend you do it away from any contacts. If I were you, I'd base myself somewhere sunny. You'll need good relaxing downtime in between jobs."

It was hard to believe what I was hearing. Did they really value me that much that they were prepared to spend a small fortune on me?

"What if I don't live up to your expectations?"

"I'm not here to massage your ego, but let's just say we don't take selecting candidates lightly."

"Who would I be working for?"

"It's a bit complicated and I'll be honest with you, like any job there are positives and negatives."

"That doesn't answer my question. Whilst I appreciate this is all a bit clandestine, it would be good if you could at least give me some straight answers."

"You won't be working for any particular organisation as such, which, as I said, has good and bad points."

"Like what?"

"For instance, you won't have a boss or regular performance reviews, but at the same time you'll be working mainly on your own. You'll be given instructions and expected to carry them out."

"And what if I don't?"

"Back to this point again," he responded with a sigh. "I thought I already spelt out the alternatives."

"But what if I don't do a good job, not because I haven't tried, but I have a bad day or make a mistake?" He laughed at this point.

"People who make mistakes in this line of work don't last very long."

I instinctively swallowed hard at hearing this, but he picked up on my reaction immediately.

"You don't need to worry; the training you'll receive, along with the skills you've already acquired, should ensure 'bad days' are unlikely."

"So, tell me what happens now."

"As I said, you'll undertake some training. Once that is completed, you'll be in the field."

"Waiting for instructions?"

"Exactly."

"And in the meantime, I chose where to live?"

"All you have to do is give us the location. We'll sort out the rest."

"Don't I get to choose the exact accommodation?"

"I'm sure you'll be happy with what you're provided with. We make sure you have everything you need. It's in our interests you are comfortable and content."

It sounded very nice and I already pictured myself somewhere in the south of France, Spain, or even the Caribbean. He hadn't specified any restrictions. Although, I would have to cut all contact with my friends and family, that was clear.

"Where do I sign?" I said with a smile.

"You don't have to sign anything. It's an informal arrangement, shall we say."

"Where does all the money come from to fund this? Taxpayers?"

"You need not concern yourself with that. But the project was given adequate funding."

"OK, but before we proceed, I need to know what's been going on over the last six months?"

"Fire away, but obviously I cannot give you any details on anyone you may have met that has been involved in the programme." I thought of H. It was hard to believe he was one of them, which, if true, meant he was very good at what he did. Before I could ask my first question, he spoke again.

"In anticipation of one question, the people you have been practicing on were carefully selected." This led me to think of my ex-girlfriend, but they were once again one step ahead of me. "We throw in a job on someone you know as a test. It's a good marker on the candidate and whether they can separate work from personal life."

"What if I hadn't done it?" I said, thinking back to the

dilemma I'd had.

"Then you would have failed." I wasn't sure what this meant. Would they have left me alone or turned me over to the police? I decided it was best not to know the answer.

"So, what about McKendrick? I was convinced it was him running this."

"Although you may not believe us, we have some ethics." I smiled ruefully. "Sometimes the victims are criminals. This serves the purpose of eradicating some of the more unsavoury characters in our society, as well as setting a challenge for potential candidates. One of yours was closely known to McKendrick. It clearly upset him."

I thought back to my victims and who it might be. Donovan was my guess. It was interesting information though, and I wondered how McKendrick had known I had been the one who killed Donovan. I thought either they could have interfered here or perhaps it was someone else. As if they read my mind, they continued.

"Other targets we give to our candidates are people that may have found out a bit too much from previous ones." I couldn't help having a warm feeling that there would be someone out there receiving a picture of Kez in their P.O. Box. Whilst I resented the fact that these people owned me, I couldn't help but like the way they operated. It somehow made their proposition more attractive.

Chapter Fourteen

Six months later

I surveyed the city from my vantage point. It was grey and uninteresting. I joked to myself that I could have been given a nicer location for my first job. I wondered if I'd find myself in Eastern Europe regularly in my work. I could well imagine jobs coming up in the Middle East, but if there was one thing I had learned from my recent experiences, it was that life wouldn't be predictable. During my training, I'd given a lot of thought to what had happened before I'd been picked up in the car the night I killed McKendrick. McKendrick and his gang, Kez and Jim. Even back to Jason. Most of them were probably dead. I never worked out Kez's motivations. On one hand, she was my friend and ally, listening to my problems and providing solutions, but there were things that happened that I couldn't help think meant she was also working against me. How had McKendrick got his information? The whole thing with Jim was strange. My conclusion was she wanted to stir things up, create a drama that she could follow. It would have most likely brought about her own downfall. Although, somehow, I don't think that she would have been overly disappointed at this. I couldn't properly work her out, but I think she would have wanted her life to end dramatically; she was a destructive person. Although, I accepted that might be rich coming from me.

The target would be along any minute now if my intel was

good. I checked the rifle once more and looked through the sight. Sure enough, he rounded the corner almost exactly as expected. It was an easier job when you had good information. Planning was more simplistic. I composed myself...